SOMEWHERE BETWEEN DANDELIONS

SOMEWHERE BETWEEN DANDELIONS

Trisha Larson Harmon

Published by Possibility Publishing

Printed in the United States.

Paperback (P.O.D.): 979-8-9900528-8-8

Kindle: 979-8-9900528-9-5

For Brooke, my sister and biggest fan who made me promise to dedicate my first book to her.

I never forgot.

For Zoey and Hunter, you are the loves of my life.

CHAPTER 1

Wishes don't come true.

Not the ones made on candles pushed into birthday cakes or those whispered in the dark with hands pressed together. Especially not the ones made on dandelions. Yet here I was—once again—being pulled forward by my ache for something more. I stepped onto the grass, my shoes sinking into the soft dirt, still moist from the recent and rare California rains, and reached for the puffed-up dandelion just off the path.

I spun the soft green stem around eyeing the perfection of the individual spores. Raising it to my mouth, I pictured Finn's familiar face then twisted the stem between my fingers and blew until all the tiny white parachutes spun away on the breeze. Once again, my hope was in the hands of the universe to do or not do with it as it wanted.

With the empty stem tucked between my fingers, I returned to the sidewalk. Absence floated beside me like a shadow as I followed the splintered cracks in the pavement on the way to my locker. The sound of Finn's voice calling goodbye to someone drifted in my direction, interrupting my thoughts. Before I could catch a glimpse of him, he was beside me.

The dandelion in my hand was barely cold from my wish—one wrong move could jinx everything. I pretended not to notice him.

"Goodnight?"

Finn was the only person who called me this and had since third grade. When the teacher called "Claire Goodnight" during roll call, Finn had turned in his seat, searching for the girl with the strange last name. Later at recess he told me my last name was cool and asked if he could call me that instead of Claire. With a slight nod, I'd granted him permission. A crooked-toothed smile filled his face and as he ran away to the playground, he pulled a piece of my heart with him.

Now, after nearly ten years of avoiding each other's eyes, we stood face to face.

He smiled and my heart somersaulted. "Are you alone?"

"Um, yes?"

"I meant are you meeting someone?"

I shook my head.

He glanced to his feet then back up again. "Do you mind if I walk with you?"

"No." Goosebumps raced over my skin and, even with the cool breeze, sweat rose from my pores.

"You've been alone this year." His long legs fell into pace with mine as I began to walk again.

His words stung and I didn't reply.

"I mean Julia moved away—right?"

My face relaxed. "You noticed that?"

"I did."

My best and only friend moving over the summer had knocked me off balance and now, halfway through senior year, I still hadn't found my center. I'd give almost anything to have her back, but without her I'd rather be alone.

"Did you have a question about the English homework?" I asked. That was the only class we shared.

"English homework?" He scrunched his eyebrows. "No."

"Oh?"

"I'm on my way to meet someone. It looks like we're going the same way."

In the curious expressions and low whispers fluttering around us I imagined everyone wondering why Finn Peterson was with me instead of Kelly McIntyre—my least favorite person. Up until a few days ago, she'd been Finn's girlfriend. My stomach twisted whenever she pranced around, all bubbly with her shiny blond ponytails, wearing his letterman's jacket like she owned him. If someone like her was his type, then my introspective ways and wavy brown hair didn't stand a chance.

I stopped at my locker. "Here I am."

"Cool," he said, but didn't turn to go.

With shaking fingers, I turned the combination lock right, left, right and pulled open the door, pretending to look for something deep inside.

He knocked, three soft taps on the metal, and I jumped, banging my head. He quickly pulled the scratched-up door all the way open, exposing me. "I didn't mean to scare you. Are you okay?"

I rubbed my head. "Yeah. Did you forget something?"

"Sort of. Actually, it was you I was looking for. I wanted to ask if you'd go out with me."

It was entirely possible this was just another one of my daydreams about Finn—but the hot flush that rushed up from my neck to my cheeks was very real.

"Um." I wanted to jump up and down, screaming *Yes!* Or more properly just smile sweetly and say "yes." Every wish I'd ever made for Finn—the boy whom I'd known, practically my whole life, but didn't really know at all—flashed through my mind. My long-time wish was finally coming true, and all I could say was "um?"

He stood still, eyebrows slightly raised, an awkward, unsure smile on his face. Had I not sensed his fear of being turned down I might've assumed I was being punked.

"You're not gonna make me ask you again, are you? The first time was hard enough." Again, his eyes shifted to his feet.

"If I promise to say yes, will you ask again?" My boldness shocked me.

His eyes brightened and he cleared his throat then, in a rush, asked. "Claire Goodnight, will you go out with me on Saturday night?"

"Okay," I said.

"That's a yes, right?" he asked.

"I promised, didn't I?"

"Can I pick you up at six?"

I had a shift Saturday night, but I wouldn't let that be an obstacle to my wish coming true.

"Okay." I wanted to smack my hand against my head to shake some more words loose.

"Okay." He laughed, volleying the word back to me.

As we exchanged numbers, our fingers touched, and prickles of electricity ran all the way to my elbow.

He walked me to my car. An uneasy silence hung in the air, but a heat radiated between us. I looked at my watch. In twenty minutes, I'd be late to work.

"You need to go?" he asked.

"Work."

"I'm headed to practice. Gotta get ready for the game tomorrow night."

"Oh, yeah," I said. "Let me text my boss real quick so he doesn't worry," I said.

I'd never been late before, and Tyler would wonder what was up if he didn't hear from me. I sensed Finn's eyes on me as I typed.

"That's a thing to text your boss?"

"He's a friend too," I said, sliding my phone into the back pocket of my jeans and noting the cloud that passed over Finn's face. Was that *jealousy*?

By now the parking lot was practically empty, and the white lines of the parking spaces stretched out around us.

He touched his finger to my nose. "See you at school tomorrow, Goodnight."

"Yes." I ached for him already. Saturday was only two days away, but that felt like forever.

He opened the door for me, and I got inside. As I drove away in my grandmother, Mimi's, old white Honda, I was reminded that this was yet another thing I wouldn't be able to tell her.

After I waved goodbye to Finn, I turned on the radio to drown out the unsettling voice telling me this was too good to be true.

CHAPTER 2

"J! You will never ever, EVER guess what just happened! Call me!"

My tires squealed as I turned into my parking space. I pulled out my ear bud and raced from my car and entered Palm Row Pizza, breathless and smiling.

The aroma of tomato sauce, cooking pizzas, and the beeping sound of the ancient Pac Man machine greeted me.

Behind the high counter, Tyler had his head bent, counting the change from the cash register. He wrote down the number on a clipboard and looked up.

"My employee finally arrives," he said, doing a double take. "Wait. You look...happy."

I rolled my eyes, but I couldn't be mad. It wasn't like I walked around with a perpetual smile on my face like Julia did, even when she was unhappy. The only time that hadn't been true was when she told me her family was moving to Oregon.

According to Julia, I'm like a turtle, always ready to retreat into my shell. But when there was no fear of danger and life was good, I emerged, and in those moments, she said I was like a butterfly. After this momentous afternoon, I was clearly in butterfly mode, but Tyler wasn't familiar with these descriptions of me.

Tyler's dark-blond hair was covered by a black baseball cap, part of our uniform and his eyes looked bluer than usual today against the dark shirt beneath his apron. Julia described him as "deliciously adorable" and said if she hadn't preferred girls, she'd date him. The sleeves of his shirt clung tightly to his arms, a sign of his recent weightlifting hobby. Had Julia been here to witness this change, I imagined she'd be calling him "Muscles."

Before Julia moved, the three of us often hung out and she'd tried convincing me to date him, telling me I couldn't wait for Finn forever. She even tried to prod Tyler into asking me out when she thought I wasn't listening. It took several months for Tyler and me to adjust from our typical party of three, to two, but the awkwardness had begun to subside.

I didn't attempt to shrink the size of my happiness. The lights were brighter, the air was easier to breathe, and my body was buoyant. "I am happy," I said.

Tyler picked up a stack of dollar bills. "You usually aren't this happy to see me, but..." He rubbed his nails on his collar like he was shining them.

I laughed. "It's not you!"

"Uh-huh, way to make a dude feel good." He turned his attention back to counting as I opened the door to the rear of the restaurant. "You might not be so happy once you get back there. Maggie called in sick this morning, so prep is behind!"

"I guess I deserve that for being late," I yelled back through the wall.

The bathroom mirror showed me what Tyler had seen— a red-cheeked, beaming girl. My dating-Finn news was bursting outwards, begging to be broadcast, but other than Julia—who I had to tell first out of loyalty—Tyler would be the only person I'd tell. Hands shaking, I checked my phone for messages. Nothing.

"J, call me at work," I typed.

I changed into my uniform and then pulled my apron over my head, wincing at the smell of caked-in grease. No matter how many times I washed them, my work clothes still reeked.

When I got to the cook table Tyler was there making a pizza, shelling out pepperoni like playing cards onto the cheese. He was right—the refrigerator was nearly empty. Normally at this time, the shelves were stocked with various crust types and prepped with sauce and cheese.

"You weren't kissing about being behind, dude!" My face flushed at my slip.

"No, I sure wasn't 'kissing'." Tyler laughed. "I told you, I've been alone all day. At least I stocked the table for you." He waved a hand towards the stainless-steel containers filled with various toppings: white cheese, pepperoni, ham, brown sausage, pineapple, jalapeños, and black olives.

"Thanks!" I laughed, grateful he hadn't teased me for my error. "Hey, do you think you can get someone to cover my shift on Saturday?" I pulled a pizza from the oven, transferred it to the cutting board, and cut it with the large rocker knife.

"You never ask me to cover your shifts."

I slid the pizza into a medium-sized box. "Something came up last minute."

"Hmmm. Something to do with why you're so happy?"

"Maybe...I haven't had a chance to tell Julia yet, so..."

"I see how it is." Tyler wiped crumbs from the counter with a cloth. "If you can get your shift covered, you can take the night off. No special treatment for friends around here! Especially now that you're looking at the new assistant manager of Palm Row Pizza."

"Really? Nice! How will you manage that with your college classes?"

"I've been handling it up until now, besides I've already been doing the work. It's more of a title thing, really."

"Congrats," I said.

He headed to the front to answer the ringing phone.

I called out after him, "Wait, doesn't being promoted by your uncle count as special treatment?"

He laughed. "We weren't talking about me!"

As I worked, waves of panic that I'd made up the whole Finn experience crept in. That morning my heart had been like a half-empty cup, now it was close to overflowing.

On my break, I made calls to co-workers and got my shift covered. With a few minutes left to spare Tyler called out to me from the front.

"Hey, Claire! J is on line two. Transferring it back."

I picked up the phone. "Finally, J! Where have you been?" I asked.

"C, if you have major news, does the fact my battery died really matter? Spill it!"

"Finn asked me out..."

"Finn Peterson?"

"Is there another one? Unbelievable, right?"

Beside me, an order began to print, and air whooshed by me as Tyler rushed around the corner.

He glanced at me. "I'll get it."

I mouthed a thank you and proceeded to gush details to Julia. Tyler was in earshot, and I knew he was listening. At least he'd know now, too.

"C! That's amaze-balls! I've never heard you so happy."

"It doesn't feel real! It's the first good thing that's happened since you left. My cheeks are sore from smiling!"

Until I had to return to work, we talked about what I should wear on my first-ever date. Always the confident one, Julia had it all figured out for me. I wasn't so sure.

The fog hung low, muting the glare from the streetlights as Tyler and I walked to the food court—an after-work ritual we'd continued after Julia left. The winter air stung my warm face, and I pulled my sweatshirt over my head as we stepped into the clouds.

Inside, I ordered a turkey sandwich and Tyler ordered a chili dog, then we sat at one of the round plastic tables.

Most of them had chairs stacked on top of them, and several mall employees sat alone, scrolling on their phones between bites of food. Mariachi music blared from one of the back kitchens. Employees with their hats turned backwards joked with each other as they wiped down counters, and mopped floors, likely hoping—as I did near closing time— that they wouldn't get any more customers.

"So, who is this Finn guy?" Tyler took a huge bite of his hot dog.

"Just a boy from school." I sipped my soda.

"Just a boy?" Tyler's gaze was steady. "You mean, just the reason you're bursting with happy?"

My cheeks flushed for what felt like the millionth time that day. "He's someone I've liked from afar for forever—you know?"

"Totally," he said, looking away.

"I never thought I'd have a chance with him." My sandwich sat untouched on the tray.

"Why is that?" he asked.

"Well, first of all, he'd been dating Kelly since tenth grade. Secondly, he's an incredibly attractive, popular basketball player and I'm...you know...just me."

"There's nothing 'just' about you, Claire. I bet you'd be surprised at how many people like you."

"Oh, I'm sure that's not true!"

"It's true. I've seen the way those pimply boys at work look at you." He laughed lightly.

My eyebrows furrowed. "Never noticed. As my friend, though, aren't you biased?"

"Maybe we all see what you don't." He wiped away orange chili smudges from the corner of his lips.

Tyler didn't usually talk to me like this—we'd always bantered back and forth, but this was different. I shrugged and pushed my sandwich away.

"You're not going to eat that?" he asked.

"Nope. Want it?"

He patted his stomach. "You know me. I can always eat. Besides, the roomies and I haven't grocery shopped in weeks."

After he had finished eating, he walked me to my car. "I'll see you tomorrow?"

"Yup, I'm scheduled until eight."

"I know. I wrote the schedule." He tapped the tip of my nose with the sandwich. "You are great, you know?"

Guilt raced through me, as I remembered Finn doing the same thing earlier. What was up with Tyler tonight?

"Oh, knock it off!" I punched his shoulder.

"Learn to take a compliment," Tyler said.

I unlocked my car door, hiding my eye roll.

"Friends say nice things to each other. I know you don't have many, but it's something they do."

"Ouch." I turned to glare at him.

"I didn't mean that the way it sounded."

"Yeah. See you later." I got in the car and closed the door hard.

"Claire." Tyler bent down, looking through my window.

I forced a smile and turned the key, letting it grind a bit.

He stepped back, clearing space for me to leave. I didn't look in the rear-view mirror to see if he was watching me go, nor did I wave to him like I had with Finn that afternoon. At this time Saturday night, Finn and I would be together, and that was the only thing that mattered.

CHAPTER 3

Cheering, whistle blows, and shoe squeaks echoed from beneath the double doors and floated on the cool night breeze. Even though Finn had invited me, I stood outside, building up the courage to go in.

Before I could pull the handle, the door opened and a man walked out, cell phone pressed to his ear. I slipped inside. The air was musky and warm. According to the scoreboard, the game was in the last quarter with only about five minutes left. Home: 58. Guest: 64.

I hunched over, making my way up the metal bleachers to the only spot I could find. When I sat down, Finn was bouncing the ball at the free-throw line.

A brown-haired woman in front of me leaned forward and yelled, "Come on, Finn, you got this!"

Finn's sister, Violet, a sophomore at Palm Row High, shushed her. "Mom, remember a few minutes ago when you promised you'd stop yelling so loud?"

The cheerleaders chanted. "Aim, shoot, put it through the hoop. Let's go, Finn!"

I blocked out Kelly McIntyre's booming cheer and crossed my fingers as Finn released the ball. It went in. Everyone around me stood up, clapping, and screaming, his mother the loudest. On the court, Finn swayed back and forth, his body a rolling wave with his arms stretched high in the air.

"He's doing his happy dance again. God, he's more embarrassing than you, Mom!" Violet said.

"Sorry, I'm late, ladies. What did I miss? And just so you know I could hear you screaming from the parking lot." Finn's dad sat down next to Mrs. Peterson and put his arm around her. When she turned to him and pecked him on the lips, I looked away, surprised by the envy I felt seeing that Finn had two loving parents, and a sibling—something I'd never had.

Finn made several more shots, leading our team to a victory, as both Finn's mom and dad cheered louder than anyone else.

After the game ended, Violet took off to talk to friends and his parents quickly made their way down the stairs. I waited until the crowd dispersed before walking down to join them.

Finn stood with his parents at the edge of the court. Sweat slipped down his temples as he guzzled water from a bottle. He grinned when he saw me.

"Hey, Goodnight." He stepped toward me and gave me an awkward side hug. "Sorry, I dripped on you." He lightly touched his finger to my cheek, wiping away his sweat.

My body erupted in goosebumps. "Thanks," I mumbled. "Good game."

His dad cleared his throat beside us. I looked up to see Finn's parents mouthing my last name to each other.

Finn laughed. "Obvious much? Mom and Dad, this is Claire Goodnight."

I repositioned my T-shirt to cover the blotchy, nervous rash creeping up from my chest to my neck. "Hello," I said, taking their hands in turn. "Nice to meet you."

His mom smiled at me, holding my gaze with her deep blue eyes. "You too, honey."

"All right, Molly, let's give them some space. See you at home, son."

"Finn, come on, man!" Finn's teammate and best friend yelled.

Finn turned. "I'll be right there, Dave."

Finn sighed. "We can't leave until the coach gives us a run-down of how we did. Wait for me?"

"Sorry, I can't. I need to get home, I have some things to do."

Finn frowned, slightly.

"I'll see you tomorrow though?"

"Yeah," he said. "Is six still good for you?"

"It's perfect."

I watched him run to the locker room like some sort of graceful, leaping animal. My heart leapt, too, at the thought of him being mine.

At home, the sound of the TV in the living room surprised me. The kitchen was just as it was when I left for school that morning, the sink piled high with dishes and the trash can close to overflowing. Sighing, I heavily placed the grocery bags on the kitchen counter beside an empty Tupperware container. The sticky note with my name on it still clung to the lid next to it.

Lisa wasn't usually home on Friday nights. My typical plan to clean the night away clearly wasn't going to happen tonight. Ripping off the note, I peeked around the corner. Surprisingly, she was alone, wine glass in hand, wearing sweatpants, her face scrubbed, free of makeup.

Holding the note out for her to see, I said. "I was saving

that food for myself, and it was definitely labeled this time."

She looked up, eyes glassy. "Oh, I didn't notice."

"Of course, you didn't."

She gulped the rest of the wine and reached forward grabbing the half-empty bottle from the coffee table. "There wasn't any other food here."

"And you couldn't go out and buy some?"

She looked back at the TV. "I've had a really crappy day."

I nodded. "Right." Not caring to know why, I returned to the kitchen and proceeded to loudly put the groceries away. Once finished I turned on the hot water in the sink, full blast, trying to drown out everything about being here with her.

After squirting excessive amounts of soap all over the crusty dishes, I began scrubbing. Once I was sure the dishwasher could handle what remained on the plates, I roughly placed them inside the machine next to the dishes I'd used that week.

Lisa didn't come into the kitchen until I'd finished cleaning up. She held an empty wine bottle and a pile of mail. The top envelope read "Past Due" in bold lettering, and I knew my latest paycheck wouldn't make it into my savings account after all.

"They let me go today," she said, not looking at me.

I snorted. "At least your temp job lasted longer than what like five months this time?"

She tossed the mail on the counter. "My final check wasn't big enough to cover the cost of these bills. I'm going to apply for unemployment, but until that comes through, I'll need you to pay these."

I shuffled through the bills—gas, electricity, and Wi-Fi were things I needed. As I'd done numerous times before, I would pay the bills and the required late fees too.

Rolling my eyes, I said, "This is insanely unfair. You know things like this never would've happened if Mimi were still alive."

"Well, it did and she's not."

"Once I graduate, I'll be out of here so fast, and you'll have to handle everything yourself."

She ignored me and walked toward the stairs leading to the second floor where our bedrooms were.

"Thanks so much, daughter, for helping pay the bills I should be paying," I muttered, once she was out of earshot.

Clutching my phone and earbuds with one hand, I grabbed the trash strings with the other. The door to the backyard slammed shut behind me. After tossing the bag, I kicked the large plastic can until my toes began to hurt. Hot, uninvited tears rushed down my cheeks. I flicked them away as I headed to the corner of the backyard where my willow tree stood, steady and predictable. With the branches floating around me, the glint of the moon, and the silence of the night, there was hope, if only fleeting, for a better life.

CHAPTER 4

At 5:55 the next night, I stood waiting for Finn at the end of my driveway wearing the jeans, black sweater, and boots Julia highly suggested I wear. I could see Lisa inside through the window with an unfamiliar man. She poured wine glass number one for him and by the way she swayed as she did it, it was at least her fourth. Why hadn't I thought to at least close the curtains? A car turned the corner and headed in my direction. My stomach whirled. Maybe he wouldn't see her.

Finn parked flush to the curb and walked around to where I stood. The smell of his still damp hair, brushed away from his freshly scrubbed skin, wafted my way.

His eyes met mine.

"Hey, Goodnight. What are you doing out here?"

"Waiting for you," I said, willing him not to look up at the house.

He opened my door and, placing a hand on my lower back, gestured for me to sit. "You're going to make things hard on me, aren't you?" he asked.

"What do you mean?"

Before closing the car door for me, he smiled and said, "I would've come to the door and knocked. Dad is a big believer in being chivalrous. He's had me practicing on my mom and Vi for years."

Forcing a smile, I wondered if he'd been this chivalrous with Kelly, but then pushed the thought away. This was my first date, and I didn't want her on it with me.

"Where are we going?" I asked once he was sitting beside me.

His hands shook slightly as he turned the key in the ignition. "It's a surprise!"

After a short drive we arrived at my neighborhood park. "Here we are," he said.

I looked around. "Is there a hidden restaurant here that I didn't know about?"

He laughed. "Sort of. I hope you like spaghetti?"

I wanted to say I'd eat anything if it meant being with him, but the only thing that came out of my mouth was, "Uh-huh."

"Thank God because that's the only option at this restaurant."

"Are we having a spaghetti picnic?"

He nodded, smiling. "Maybe? Stay there, I'm coming around to get you."

On the passenger side of the car, he held out his hand. I placed my hand in his and my fingers buzzed. He didn't let go as he led me to a table several feet away.

It was as if I'd stepped onto a set of one of the Netflix movies Julia and I watched together. The table was set like an Italian restaurant with a white and red checkered tablecloth. Silverware was wrapped with cloth napkins beside place settings. Candles flickered in the dimming light, casting shadows on the surrounding trees.

He squeezed my hand. "Is it too much?"

I squeezed back, reassuring both of us. "You did all of this for me?"

"Yes."

A warmth I'd never experienced spread through my chest. "It's amazing," I said.

Our eyes met and my whole body sparked.

"I'm glad you like it. Take a seat."

I sank onto a cushion resting on the bench. Finn opened a container and spooned spaghetti and meatballs onto the plate before me—steam danced ghost-like into the air.

"Did you have help with this?"

He smiled, "Maybe a little."

"Thank you," I said.

"You're welcome, Goodnight."

My stomach was already full of butterflies, and I ate timidly attempting to keep sauce off my face. Everything tasted amazing and I was reminded that the last true home-cooked meal I'd had was at Julia's house a week before she moved away.

After a few moments, I finally blurted what I'd been thinking since the moment he asked me out. "Can you tell me why?"

Finn looked at me over the candles, his face haloed in light. "Why what?"

I pretended to wipe my face, hiding my nervous expression behind the napkin, "Why you asked me out."

"It's hard to explain."

"We have nothing but time," I said.

He took another bite, appearing to think as he chewed. After he swallowed, he said, "Well, Kelly was easy..."

Shocked, I quickly stood up. The next few seconds passed in slow motion as one leg caught on the bench, and I fell backward. My boot snagged onto the plastic tablecloth pulling half the items on the table down with me. I hit the ground with a thud as spaghetti flew up and landed on my face and hair.

"Claire!" Finn called.

My face burned. I attempted to get up but couldn't.

"Are you okay?" he asked, grabbing my hands to help me sit up.

Wishing I could undo this moment, I said. "Not really."

"Are you hurt?"

"Not physically," I muttered, untangling my legs from the bench.

Just then I noticed one of the glass-encased candles, still burning, tilted on its side on the grass. "The candle!"

Finn scooped it up and held it near my face to see me better. "There goes dinner."

I reached up and pulled noodles from my hair. "It might still be edible."

He laughed. "Wait, did you think I meant Kelly was easy like *easy?*"

"Maybe?"

He blushed then mumbled. "Well, we did do it, but that's not what I meant."

I tried to get up and he grabbed my arm. "Wait! I want to explain this to you."

Sinking back into the grass, I nodded.

"What I meant was Kelly was easy to be with because we were in the same circles at school. I was the basketball player, and she was the cheerleader. You know when I moved back to Cali in tenth grade?"

"Mm-hmm." Of course, I knew. He'd moved to Arizona and was gone for three years, I thought I'd never see him again.

"She began flirting with me right away and it'll sound lame, but I wanted to fit in again and all of my friends on the team were dating cheerleaders...so I just let it happen."

I recalled the moment Kelly had turned in her seat and introduced herself to Finn on his first day back. I'd sadly witnessed their beginning and, in my mind, our end. Without knowing it, Kelly had killed any chance I might've had with Finn, and I may not have known her, but I hated her for it.

"Things were decent between us, but when she started making college plans and assumed we'd go to the same place, it freaked me out. I didn't mean for us to be forever."

I turned away from him, trying to see beyond the darkness of the night surrounding us as my heart pulled inside its turtle shell.

He cleared his throat. "Goodnight. Say something."

Sighing, I said, "What does that have to do with me?"

He shuffled beside me and before I knew it, he was gripping my hands in his.

"I have more to say if you're willing to hear it."

I nodded but pulled my hands away. His face dropped.

"You know how you just said, we have nothing but time?"

"Yes?"

"Well, I'm not sure I do. I woke up one day last week, sweating, with the thought that I didn't have much time left, and I was wasting what I did have. It was as if I'd had blinders on and suddenly, they'd been ripped off. I started paying attention to other couples and how they acted. I never found myself staring at Kelly like Dave does with his girlfriend. Then, and this is where you come in, I realized there was someone I'd caught myself looking at that way…"

My breath hitched. If he didn't say me, I'd probably slap him.

"I broke up with Kelly because staying with her wasn't fair to either of us anymore. Then I started smiling at this girl, whenever I saw her. For three days in a row, she looked away without returning my smile, then on the fourth day, she smiled back. The girl with the cool last name *finally* smiled at me."

My heart softened and even if I wanted to stop the smile that took over my face, I don't think I could've.

His eyes lit up.

I snorted, "I smile."

"The only time I saw you smile was when you were with Julia. You never smiled at me."

How had I never smiled at him? But I knew he was right. There was no possible way he could've known about my long-time crush on him. I'd never once done anything to show my interest in him.

"I don't want easy. I want you."

I giggled but said, "You don't know me."

"You don't know me either. Maybe you won't even like me."

"I'm not sure that's possible," I said.

He smiled, "For now, we have time, right? Or are you going away for college?"

"My goal has always been to leave Palm Row…"

His smile faded. "Oh."

"We have now," I said, reaching for his hand.

"Around you I always got butterflies," he said, squeezing my hand. "She never gave me butterflies."

"Can we not talk about her, ever again?" I asked.

"Strike my last statement from the record! Sorry, my dad is a lawyer," he laughed.

He was so close now, I wondered if he could hear my heart thumping against my chest.

"My turn to ask a question," he said.

"Okay."

"Why do you go to my basketball games?"

I blushed but smiled slightly. "I don't go to basketball games."

He scrunched his eyebrows. "Hmm. You must have a twin then. Come on, Goodnight! I've been honest with you!"

"Isn't it obvious?"

"Nothing about you is obvious."

I shook his shoulders. "I went to see you play because I like you," I said. My words floated between us, finally free.

"Ah-ha! How long have you liked me?"

"Since you knocked me off that swing in kindergarten. You probably don't remember that…"

He smiled. "How could I forget? I don't think anyone has ever glared at me like you did that day. That's such a long time. How did we not get here sooner?"

"Seems you had blinders on, and I've just been waiting."

He studied me for a long moment. "I'm going to have to kiss you tonight."

My face flushed. "I'm going to have to let you."

Finn stood and pulled me up with him then wrapped his arms around me. His heart pounded in thick bursts against mine. We held each other in silence, our beats syncing up.

My heart stood at attention, working out this new emotion. In the span of an hour my whole world had shifted. I wanted to soak him up, let him into my life, and not be without him ever again. I wondered how couples existed apart from each other.

I didn't want to wait anymore. Pulling back from his chest I stood on tiptoes and kissed his cheek. His smile bloomed against my face. He turned to me, and our lips timidly pressed together, puzzle pieces clicking into place. My brain screamed *first kiss, first kiss!* I had no clue what I was doing, but my body knew, meeting him as he met me, no lessons required.

Finn rubbed slow circles on my back. Our mouths opened and closed against each other's. Our tongues were warm and sticky with longing. He lightly kissed my top lip, then my bottom lip, and I returned the motion. Had he not been holding me, I would've drifted away.

We untangled, heaving for breath, our eyes meeting. Finn sighed and put his hands on my cheeks.

"Thank you," I whispered.

"What are you thanking me for?"

"I know it's not your first anything—but this is my first—everything," I said.

"I'm glad it was with me."

We moved into each other once more, losing time. After several minutes, we pulled back again. Finn spread out a blanket on the grass. I rested my head on his chest, and we stared up at a starry sky made just for us, holding onto each other like we'd never let go.

Time stretched out, passing too quickly. Our lips met again, and we kissed the breath out of each other. I sank deeper into his kisses, cementing them to memory so I could replay this night over and over.

Later, after Finn dropped me off, I walked inside with the pressure of him still on my lips, the pricks of his facial hair on my skin, and a terrible feeling that this was too good to be true.

CHAPTER 5

Standing outside English class, on Monday morning, I willed my phone to vibrate. Hours had passed since my last text to Finn. Still no reply. Any minute he'd turn the corner, smiling when he saw me with a perfect excuse for his delay. When he didn't appear, dread bubbled within me.

Inside the classroom, Finn's desk was the only one empty, and like a spotlight directed at the action in a dark theatre, it was all I could see. I sat heavily on my seat. Ms. Duncan pulled the door closed. Her heels clicked across the floor.

Something wasn't right.

My mind rattled off reasons for his absence. Maybe his car broke down or he'd woken up feeling too sick to come to school. But those things wouldn't have prevented him from texting me.

When Ms. Duncan called my name during roll call, I half raised my hand. If Finn wasn't "here," I didn't want to be either.

As Ms. Duncan neared his name my heartbeat quickened.

"Finn?" She looked up. "Hmm." She made a mark on her paper before moving on.

The meaning of his absence was lost on everyone but me.

I zoned out and checked my phone repeatedly. It remained notification-free. A knowing pulled at my heart, believing in a happily ever after for me and Finn had been stupid.

Halfway through the period a kid in the back of the room gasped, then whispered something to someone. There was another gasp.

"Care to share what's going on back there?" the teacher asked.

"It's...um. This is insane," the boy said. "I was scrolling on Facebook—sorry, Ms. D—and there's this post from Finn's best friend, David..."

My neck swiveled owl-like toward the sound of Finn's name. The blood in my veins stopped flowing. I gripped the edge of my desk.

A girl in the front row looked at her phone. "Oh, my God."

"What's happened?" someone asked.

"He's dead," someone else said.

I never spoke in class unless I'd been called upon, but now I screamed, "Who's dead?"

"Finn," the boy at the back of the room said.

The class erupted into a flurry of noise and movement.

"He was fine on Friday," someone said.

"He was. I saw him then, too."

"No way," another voice said.

I snatched the phone out of the hand of the person next to me and read the post.

David Thomas feeling heartbroken

I can't believe it. I'm in complete shock. Finn died in his sleep last night. This doesn't feel real. I love you forever, man. #RIPFinn

My ears buzzed. The words reached inside me like hands, plucking out my heart and tearing it into two uneven, bloody pieces before shoving it back inside, forever changed.

"This isn't some sort of prank, is it?" Ms. Duncan asked.

"Who would joke about something like that?" the boy asked.

"Okay, okay, let's settle down," she said.

No one did.

I dropped the phone on my desk. It bounced then clattered to the floor.

"Hey!" The owner bent to pick it up.

I grabbed my stuff and stood, pushing my way through the aisle, kicking feet and backpacks. A wail seared through the hallway as I exited the classroom. I raised my hand to my mouth to be sure the screech wasn't coming from me, but my jaw was clenched.

Kelly's back was pressed against a wall. Her hands clutched at her hair, friends surrounding her. My empty stomach wrenched. I envied her outward release, the comfort she instantly received, and the fact that everyone knew how much Finn meant to her. Now no one would know what he meant to me. I covered my ears and ran from her shrieks.

He was so alive. There'd been no warning of this, only the voice inside my head telling me it was too good to be real.

Like that Emily Dickinson quote, my hope for what Finn and I could've been no longer had feathers. It had crashed to the ground. Dead like him.

Yards from where Finn had asked me out, I dropped to my knees and threw up the little bit I'd eaten that morning. As I wiped my mouth, I noticed two dandelions side by side—mocking me—maybe they were just weeds like Lisa had always said. Pulling them from the ground, I squished them in my fist, then shredded them to pieces with my fingers, and tossed their remains in with my vomit. F dandelions. F everything.

How could he just be gone?

In my car, the world spun around me. I held onto the wheel, going nowhere. Bells rang, classes resumed, then ended. My internet searches were useless. There was no new information about Finn or what had taken him away from me.

I remained in my car until the school day ended, and the parking lot was empty. It was as if everyone else had given up that maybe he would show up after all. Driving away wouldn't make me feel better or change the fact that Finn was…gone, but I couldn't stay there forever. Instead, I got out of my car and began to run. Not stopping until I reached the empty field, acres, and acres wide, a few blocks away from home.

I stumbled through the dirt and weeds, the sharp sticks scratched at my ankles and caught on my socks. I tripped over the uneven ground filled with gopher holes but didn't stop running until my chest heaved.

Tears raced down my cheeks and snot ran from my nose. I rubbed my sweatshirt across my face, breathing in and out in short, quick bursts.

Then, there in the middle of the forgotten field, I released my own screams—louder, angrier, and more broken than Kelly's.

I bent down and picked up handfuls of dirt, pebbles, and weeds. Then spun around, tossing it all away like tiny grenades. Screaming skyward, "Why do you take everyone away?!"

In response, the clouds slowly floated across the blue sky as if nothing had changed. The Earth had continued to rotate after Mimi died and it wouldn't stop for Finn either.

The weight of it all pulled me down, and my knees hit the dirt with a thud. Closing my eyes against the glaring sun, I curled into the fetal position. In the dark of my mind, memories of Finn rushed forward. His five-year-old face hovering over me, his hand held out to help me up after knocking me off the swing. All the times we passed each other in the hallways, the times I'd purposely-accidentally bumped into him, his face when he asked me out, his hand in mine, his eyes right before our first kiss, his arms around me.

Memories of Mimi wasting away too fast for me to process also shoved their way into the flood. Mimi's loss had drilled a hole deep inside me that I'd filled with anger at her for not telling me she was dying, but I'd had years of living with her. I'd lost Finn right before we'd ever really had a chance to become something. I didn't know what was worse—having loved and lost someone or having lost someone I never had a chance to love. My body shook with crying, and it didn't stop until I finally fell asleep on the unforgiving ground.

When I opened my eyes hours later the sun had moved across the sky and was close to fading beneath the horizon. My eyes were nearly swollen shut and my face burned hot.

I pulled my phone from my jeans pocket and went to Google again. This time several articles popped up when I entered Finn's name. They all said a version of the same thing. He was described as a well-liked, star basketball player who was known to be healthy, yet for some unknown reason he hadn't woken up that morning. Foul play wasn't suspected, and the cause of death was pending an autopsy.

All I wanted was for Finn to hold me like he had on Saturday night, like I'd imagined him doing for the rest of my life.

Going home would bring me no comfort and Julia would worry too much if I called her now. Tyler was my only option. I texted him. His reply asking where he should meet me was immediate.

As the deep orange sun melted away, Tyler's headlights cut through the darkness and the sound of his door slamming shut broke the silence.

"Claire!" he yelled. "Where are you?"

"Here," I said, but the screaming, crying and lack of water had taken my voice. Turning on the flashlight on my phone, I waved it in the air, signaling my location. He moved toward me, barely a shadow in the dusk.

"Claire, what's going on?" He knelt in front of me. "Are you okay?"

I kept my head down and picked at my fingernails. The only sound came from the crickets. Why wouldn't they shut up?

"I'll kill him if he did something to hurt you," Tyler said.

"He's already dead," I said. The words echoed through me.

"What?" Tyler grabbed my hands; they were warm against the coldness of mine. I didn't squeeze back, but I didn't pull away.

"I don't understand how he could just be gone." My voice, barely a whisper, didn't sound like mine.

"Claire, I'm so sorry. How long have you been out here?"

I looked up at him and his eyes searched mine in the near dark, back and forth.

More tears streaked down my face.

"Oh, God, Claire," he said. He shifted and pulled me toward him. His body heat pressed up against my damp sweatshirt. I'd been numb to the cold closing in around me but now I began shaking. He squeezed me harder, and it made me cry more—the ghost of Finn's touch still so present.

"I've got you, Claire," he said. "Can I take you somewhere?"

"My car is still at school, and I don't want to go home," I said.

"Okay, alright—we'll go to my place."

I nodded into him, attempting to unfold my legs, and gasped at the instant shock of pain. "My feet are asleep."

"Can I carry you?" he asked, and after my brief nod he scooped me up.

The darkness grew thick around us. My phone flashlight was still on. I held it out, illuminating a shaky path for us.

The feeling returned to my legs as Tyler drove to his place.

At his front door, he stopped and asked. "You remember the roommates I've told you about?"

"Yes," I said.

"I don't know what it looks like in there right now. Just, don't hold it against me—cool?"

I nodded.

"I have the master bedroom to myself. We can hang out there."

Julia and I had never been to Tyler's house, and I briefly wondered why. A large flat screen TV was attached to a wall. Two mismatched couches sat around a coffee table cluttered with soda cans and fast-food trash. The light-brown carpet had several odd-shaped stains on it.

He surveyed the room. "Not as bad as it could've been."

A door to the left of us opened and a hairy-chested guy in boxer shorts came out of a bathroom, the sound of a toilet flushing behind him.

"Give a guy a heads-up, man!" he said when he saw us.

"Sorry, Matt, I didn't expect you'd be hanging all out like that," Tyler said, laughing.

"Whatever," Matt said, picking up a pair of jeans from a pile on the floor and putting them on. He stepped toward me and held out his hand. "Hello, nice to meet you."

"Whoa!" Tyler warned. "Don't even think about touching her—I know you don't wash your hands."

Matt held them up, "They're washed. Probably even still a bit wet."

"Let's spare her that," Tyler said.

I dropped my outstretched hand.

"This is Claire," Tyler said. "We work together."

"Hi, Claire. I think you've been mentioned around here, no...?" Matt eyed Tyler with raised eyebrows.

Tyler shrugged. "Maybe in passing."

"Are you alright? You look sort of tore up," Matt said.

My appearance didn't matter at all to me, but I lifted my hand to my hair and felt knots and sticks.

"She's all good, man." Tyler put his hand on my lower back and led me to a room at the end of a short hallway. He flipped a light switch on and closed the door behind us.

Tyler's bed was crumpled with twisted beige sheets and a blue bedspread. A laptop sat open on his desk, the screen blank. Tyler picked up some clothes from the floor, threw them into his closet, and began making his bed. I'd never been in a guy's bedroom before. It had a mixture of smells: sweat, cologne, and dust.

"Sorry, I wasn't expecting company," he said.

"I don't care. This day has been unexpected in every way." The pit in my stomach was growing deeper.

I lowered myself onto the bed. He pulled up the chair from his desk and sat down.

My hands were scratched and dirty, small bruises already beginning to form. Sand and dirt pressed up against my toes inside my shoes.

I wanted Finn.

"A shower or a bath might help you feel better. I have a surprisingly nice bathtub in there." He gestured toward the bathroom door.

I doubted anything could wash away the sadness caked all over me, but I nodded.

"Cool. Let me clean up the bathroom a bit and get you some clothes to change into."

I stared ahead, seeing nothing.

"I put a sweatshirt, sweatpants, and a fresh towel in there for you. I found a bottle of shampoo and conditioner that an ex left here that you can use. I only have men's body wash, but you can use it to clean yourself and for bubbles in the tub if you want. That's what I do."

His mention of an ex briefly piqued my attention, but it quickly faded.

I cleared my dry throat. "Thanks."

Thanking him reminded me of thanking Finn on our date. Everything reminded me of him.

"Oh! Let me get you some water. Have you eaten?"

I shook my head. My stomach was empty, but I didn't feel hungry.

"I'll go pick up some food for us. I'll have Matt come with me to pick up your car if that's okay."

"Thank you," I mumbled, pulling the keys from my pocket.

I heard him speak briefly with his roommate before coming back in with two bottles of water. "They aren't cold," he said.

"It's okay," I said.

"Take as long as you need. Lock the doors. Not that anyone would come in, but just so you feel safe."

My desire for warmth and comfort won over the discomfort of being naked in an unfamiliar place. I sat at the edge of the oversized tub and turned on the water, letting it fill up a third of the way before liberally adding in the body wash. The bubbles caught the light, rainbows encased inside, but I refused to let my mind declare it beautiful.

I peed, then drank one of the water bottles quickly, glad it wasn't cold. I opened the other one and had a few sips. The mirror confirmed that I looked how I felt.

Bubbles snapped around me as I sank into the tub. Hot water stung the nicks on my hands and ankles. This was only a minor distraction from the pain in my heart. Head against the tub, I waited for the filth of the field to slip off my skin.

The smell, of course, reminded me of Tyler. It was the scent he always carried with him. Occupied with something controllable, I dug dirt out from beneath my fingernails. I washed and rinsed my hair with Tyler's ex's shampoo. He'd never mentioned any girls to me, but I suppose I'd never asked. I'd learned from him that guys didn't tend to offer up information unless directly asked about it.

Sometime later, after I was clean and wrapped in a towel, I watched the dirty water drain. My heart begged for more tears, but my body lacked the energy to make them. Once my body was dry, I dressed in the clothes Tyler left me. The sweatpants were too big, and I had to fold them at my waist several times to prevent them from falling off. His sweatshirt hung loose and large but was perfect for disappearing into. He'd also left me a pair of socks and they stretched up to just below my knees. I found a comb in a drawer and forced it through my tangled hair.

My phone vibrated. For a second, I hoped it was from Finn, but no, just Tyler. He asked me to let him know when I was ready for him to come back in. I replied. A moment later he was knocking on his own bedroom door.

Stepping inside with two wooden TV trays, he said, "Hey."

"Hey."

After he'd set them up, he picked up a white bag of food and a cup holder filled with drinks that had been waiting in the hallway.

"Take a seat, madam," he said.

My stomach rumbled.

"I wasn't sure what to get you, but you can never go wrong with burgers and fries, right?"

He unwrapped a cheeseburger and placed it in front of me, shook out a few fries, and set the bag down next to the burger.

"And two drink options—a chocolate shake and hot chocolate."

The hot chocolate might help soothe my tattered throat, so I went with that. Then I took a juicy bite of the cheeseburger, chewing while he set up his own food.

Unused to anyone anticipating my needs, I hadn't even known what I'd needed, but everything he offered made me feel more human. Mimi had taken care of me, but mainly focused on teaching me how to take care of myself. Since she died, I'd become used to doing that.

He held out two small cups. "Ketchup or ranch?"

"Hmm, both?"

"A mixer, huh?" He took the lids off and placed them on my tray.

My small laugh sounded foreign, and I instantly wanted to take it back. *Undo. Undo.* It didn't feel right to laugh when Finn no longer could.

We didn't speak. Tyler downed every bite and ate what I didn't. I leaned against his headboard, sipping the hot chocolate.

He disappeared with the trash and came back wiping his hands on his jeans. "Do you mind if I sit?"

"It's your bed," I said.

"Right, but I don't want to make you uncomfortable." He sat next to me, leaving a safe distance between us on the queen-sized bed.

"Oh, thanks. You're being very sweet," I said. It wasn't often that I complimented anyone, and the words were out before I'd thought them. I looked at him briefly, his blue eyes concerned and so close, before distracting myself with the strings on the hood of the sweatshirt.

"Anytime, Claire, you know that. Do you want to talk?"

"Not really. I mean, I don't know. It doesn't seem real, but I feel so sad." There were the tears again, rushing hot and fat down my face, rolling onto my neck.

He moved closer, putting his arm around me. "I wish I could take away your pain."

I cried in his arms for a long time. Finally, he broke the silence with, "Your hair smells nice."

"The ex-girlfriend scent," I said. Once again, I wanted to pull the words out of the air and erase them.

A laugh rumbled in his chest. "Funny," he said.

"You never told us about a girlfriend," I said, shifting out of his arms and leaning back against the pillow.

"Not much to tell," he said. "But we aren't talking about me." He waved his hand, closing the subject. "How can I help you? Do you want some time off work?"

The whole life-going-on-without-Finn thing slammed into me again. I worked a lot so I could save money to escape Lisa, but Finn was dead. Saving money didn't seem important anymore. Going away didn't seem as urgent. Nothing did.

"You never take time off, Claire. It's okay."

Even though work would be a distraction, I didn't want to return to life as normal as I had done after Mimi. Not yet. "Time off sounds good, actually," I said.

"I'll cover your shifts for a week. Then you can let me know if you want more time."

"Thank you," I said.

"You don't have to thank me. You can stay the night if you want. I can sleep on the couch in the front room or on the floor in here, whatever works for you."

"I would like to stay," I said, meeting his relieved gaze. "You can sleep here. We'll just stay on our own sides of the bed."

"Absolutely," he said. "Do you want to call Julia or your mom?"

"Julia should know, but I don't feel like explaining anything right now. Lisa isn't someone I want to talk to about this," I said. My eyes felt heavy, and I laid my head on the pillow and closed my eyes, ending the conversation. I didn't need anyone to comfort me—no one could take this ache away.

Later, Tyler snored softly next to me, and it took me hours to fall asleep. Dreams of Finn's face coming toward mine repeated throughout the night.

Close to six am, the light peeked in through the blinds. I woke up with my head on Tyler's chest and his arm curved around my back. The bed squeaked beneath me as I shifted out from under him, not wanting to wake him. In the bathroom, I changed into yesterday's clothes, folded the borrowed ones, and placed them on the counter. I grabbed my car keys from Tyler's nightstand, crept out of his room, and quietly closed the front door of the apartment after me. Then without choice, I began a new day of living in a world without Finn.

CHAPTER 6

Existing without Finn felt like being on the moon— endless and empty. Reminders of him were everywhere—at my locker, in the parking lot, the curb outside my house, and then there were the dandelions. More than once I thought I saw him walking the hallways and my heart plummeted each time like a skydiver with a broken parachute when I realized it wasn't him.

Julia's parents had offered to fly her out to spend a weekend with me.

"Tell them thank you, but I wouldn't be good company," I said.

"That's not the point," she'd said. "I can be there for you, C."

"Having you back for a couple of days for you to leave again wouldn't help me." Losing someone all over again would be too much.

Talking about how sad I was all the time wasn't good for either of us and as the days after Finn's death wore on, she and I spoke less and less. She loosened the leash between us, and I gratefully took the extra space, pulling into my turtle shell—keeping everyone at a distance.

Tyler checked in on me, but I hadn't let him see me cry again. Every few days he brought me dinner, and we sat in my front yard to eat. Before he drove away, I'd let him pull me into a hug. He'd read somewhere that twenty-second hugs released oxytocin and figured it was worth trying. I counted the seconds, and he was right, I felt better momentarily. On the harder days, I came to recognize when a Tyler hug would've helped, but I never asked him to make a special trip for me.

I didn't tell Lisa about Finn. She didn't care to know anything about me, and I couldn't take the rejection that opening up to her would bring. Thankfully, she booked a new temp job, but when she was home, I went outside and spent hours beneath my willow tree. Once the leafy strings surrounded me, I wrapped myself in a blanket and laid on the lawn chair. Watching the branches swing in the breeze, I tried not to beg the universe for another chance with Finn, but I always did.

As the days slowly ticked on, I reshelved my losses.

Fifteen days after he died, a school memorial was taking place. Attempting to avoid mingling with the crowd beforehand, I arrived right as it was about to start.

The theatre loomed spooky against the sunless day. Built in the late 1800s, it was the last original building remaining on campus. Reminiscent of Ancient Roman architecture, white columns framed the double doors. Inside, century-old memories lurked in the shadows. A chill swept over me, and I pulled my black cardigan tight across my chest.

Most of the theatre's blue padded seats were occupied by students in dark funeral wear. I found a spot near the back, close to the exit. The red EXIT sign burned bright in the dimly lit room, a beacon of escape. Staring straight ahead, I waited, listening to a slow piano and violin composition being played over the surround-sound speakers and willed my tears away.

A blown-up photo of Finn's school basketball picture was propped up on an easel center stage. In it, he wore his blue letterman's jacket and held a basketball under one arm. His eyes shone with laughter.

An usher wearing a black suit and tie pulled the doors closed and the music abruptly stopped. Finn's dad, mom and sister walked slowly up the stairs to the podium.

Mr. Peterson wore a gray suit and a dark blue tie. He adjusted the microphone to his height. Mrs. Peterson wore a plain black dress and a strand of white pearls that reflected the light. She stood rigid, gripping the edge of the dark wood stand. Violet wore a dark-blue dress and clutched a crumpled tissue. I looked down at my lap.

Because of Mimi's death, I knew the anger and bitterness that lurked beneath their sadness. The talk around school was that Finn's autopsy report said he'd died of a brain hemorrhage. After googling it, I'd learned that there were no signs of it, and nothing could be done to prevent it, which must've made it feel even worse.

I squeezed my hands into fists, digging my nails into my palms.

"Thank you all for coming today to honor Finn." Mr. Peterson cleared his throat. "We still haven't accepted the fact that he's gone and maybe we never will. I'd like to acknowledge those of you who have reached out with kind words and cards. To those of you who sent meals, thank you. Finn was an amazing son and big brother to Violet. We've heard many stories from you, all of him being a great friend, as well. We will miss him for the rest of our lives."

He cleared his throat again. "We had a private ceremony for Finn, but after many requests wanted to allow you an opportunity to honor him, too. I know we have several people who want to speak today. If you haven't signed up but would like to say a few words, please feel free to come up. Once again, we thank you for coming."

Finn's family moved away, and something flickered on stage. I wiped at my tears, glanced around the theatre then looked back to the stage. No one else seemed to notice the fog-like form following Violet down the stairs.

Finn's basketball coach stepped up next. His voice boomed through the large room. Finn's family sat down in the front row and the figure remained upright, looking up at Coach Walker.

Without thinking, I stood and moved to the center aisle. My seat banged as it bounced up to a folded position, but it went unnoticed or so I thought. The shape turned my way.

I tried to make sense of what I was seeing even as my brain said *Finn*.

I blinked several times, then shook my head so hard my ponytail hit the sides of my face. He was still there. The butterflies that had gone MIA the day Finn died gleefully returned, creating a small tornado in my stomach.

I squeezed my eyes shut, every ounce of my being begged for this to be real.

When I opened my eyes again, the thing was gliding through the air between us, floating above the thinning carpet with a grin on his face. Other than his white-socked feet, he wore a black hoodie and jeans. His brown hair was bed-head messy.

My mouth dropped open as our eyes met.

"Goodnight! You can see me, can't you?"

He rushed toward me, his arms out, ready to embrace me, but he went straight through me, electrifying my entire body and knocking me breathless. A buzzing rang in my ears. I tripped backward a few steps before catching myself on an empty row of seats with an "Ooof."

Several shadowed heads turned to shush me. I side-shuffled behind a column at the side of the theatre, not taking my eyes off his.

It *was* Finn.

Or had I gone crazy and created this illusion?

"This can't be real," I whispered.

He was close enough that I should've been able to smell his breath, but there was no scent.

"It is. I'm really here," he said.

He was see-through and sort of shimmery, as if he'd emerged from a movie screen.

"Don't freak out," he said.

I couldn't speak.

His eyes were wide and searching. "You're freaking out, aren't you?"

There were hundreds of people in the room, and *no one* could see Finn but me?

"This isn't happening," I said.

"It is."

"But it doesn't make sense."

He touched my hand, and sparks of energy tickled my fingers just as they had when he was alive. I pulled my hand away. As much as I wanted Finn back, this was impossible.

"You can feel me, can't you?" he asked.

Feeling crazy, I shook my hands then blinked several times. He was still there. Looking at me.

"I'm real. I can prove it," he said.

Finn walked to a row filled with people and raced through them like he was running on the basketball court. My breath caught at their reactions. Some put their hands up to their hair, some rubbed at the place Finn had grazed, one girl touched the chair in front of her, steadying herself, while others were oblivious to the change in the atmosphere.

"See, they can feel me, too." Finn grinned. "Now, can we get out of here?"

A shaky female voice began to speak into the microphone. We both turned to look. Kelly stood there wearing Finn's letterman jacket over a short black dress. She'd been wearing his jacket every day since he died, and I wanted to tear it off her.

"I would've gotten that back from her if this hadn't happened." He motioned to his ghostly form. Then said, "Follow me."

I followed him to the exit, breathing a sigh of relief that he didn't care to hear what she had to say about him, that it was me he wanted.

He walked through the door, his hand reappeared beckoning me out. I pushed it open, slipped out, and slowed its closing until it quietly clinked shut behind me.

We stood looking at each other in the light of day.

"I'd hoped it was you. I wanted to still be here for you," he said.

"Here for me? What do you mean?" I gripped the stair railing to prevent my knees from buckling.

He nodded. "I guess I have some explaining to do."

"I think I've lost my mind," I said.

"I wouldn't trick you, Goodnight."

My legs wobbled. "This doesn't make sense."

"Do you want to sit down?"

His eyes still made my heart quiver. I nodded.

We found a spot on the grass out of sight from the theatre. His gaze bore through me like he was reading everything inside me. I looked down at my hands. For the last two weeks all I'd done was think about all the things I wanted to say, but now my mind was blank.

"You can't read my mind, can you?" I asked.

"I wish, but no, I can't. So, hey, I'm sorry for ghosting you, but I do have a pretty good excuse for it, right?"

"That's only a little bit funny because you're a...ghost?"

"Yup. And that was a ghost-joke. You know like a dad-joke, but..."

"Yeah, I got that. I'm still not convinced that I don't need some sort of medical intervention, but I've never been so happy to see a ghost."

"I know it seems nuts. I get that you might need some time to adjust."

"Can you explain how this is possible?" I asked.

Finn shrugged. "I never thought much about the afterlife or ghosts, but here I am, proof that they exist."

A week after Mimi died, I thought I'd seen her waving to me, a shadow of white light, amongst the glare of the blinding sunrise. She'd lifted her hand in a wave and before I had time to blink or react, she was gone. At the time I'd explained the sighting as a hallucination, but maybe it had been real after all. Maybe she'd been giving me the goodbye she'd stolen from me by keeping her illness a secret, until it had been too late for goodbyes.

Even years later, I occasionally felt Mimi's presence, though, I'd never seen her again. There was no reason for me to not believe in ghosts, heaven, or an afterlife, especially now.

Above us the clouds separated, and the sun began to shine through the cracks, forming puzzle pieces in the sky. I had to go either all in or all out and losing him again wasn't something I'd choose.

"Okay," I said.

He smiled. "Okay. Thank you for not running away screaming."

"I'd never run away from you," I said.

"Did you already forget about our date?" He laughed.

He was right. My nerves did have escape plans. I waved my hand at him, brushing away his comment. "Why do you think you're here for me?"

"You're the only one who can see me. It has to be you I'm still here for."

"Wait, am I going to die, too? Are you here to take me to the other side with you?"

Finn laughed. "I haven't even been to the other side yet! And no, I don't think you need to worry about dying any time soon."

"Then why do you think you're here for me?"

"Can I tell you something without freaking you out?"

"Hmmm, try me," I said.

"After I died, a bright light surrounded me, and an overwhelming sense of peace and love washed over me. You still with me?" he asked.

I'd heard stories of near-death experiences that started off similarly. I nodded.

"An older woman in a long white dress appeared. She held my hands in hers and talked to me. Her voice was like a song. I swear it was like she spoke for hours, but I barely remember anything she said."

I leaned forward. "What *do* you remember?"

"She said I had more left to do here and that it would make sense once I saw *her*."

"Her?" I asked.

"Yup, just *her*. I know there isn't more than one 'her' intended, so..."

My stomach flipped. "Why me?"

He smiled. "Unfinished business, maybe?"

"How long can you stay?" I asked.

"I'm not sure. I didn't get a ghost handbook."

"We'll have to make one together."

"I'd like that," he said. "I don't want to get in your way or be a bother though."

"Are you kidding? I've been dying for you to be here." I clapped my hand over my mouth.

Finn put his hand over mine and electricity surged between us once again. "I've come to terms with being dead."

"I haven't."

"You're not the only one." His eyes turned in the direction of the theatre. "My family changed overnight. It's like I broke them."

"I know how they feel, but it's only because you mean so much. I wish you were still alive."

"I know. And believe me, if I had the power to change things and put all the broken pieces back together, I would have," he said.

"Are you really okay with this?" I gestured to his ghostly form. He didn't seem sad or angry. There was an air of acceptance about him.

"With being a ghost or being dead?"

"Both, I guess?"

"Acceptance came pretty easily. I did try jumping back into my body but obviously that didn't work. Besides, I can do cool things now." He pressed his hand through the grass, and it disappeared.

"Can you touch me again?"

He lifted his hand to mine, and we pressed our hands together. My whole body woke up, reliving how he made me feel mushy and alive. I sucked in air and pulled my hand back.

"Does it hurt?" he asked.

"No, it feels a little like being shocked, but in a good way," I said.

"Don't they always say it gets cold when ghosts are around?"

"You aren't cold. Honestly, I feel really warm around you." I placed my hands on my reddening cheeks.

"Awesome," he smiled.

"Will you be with me all the time, like twenty-four hours a day?" I asked.

"If you want me to," he said.

"That could get awkward."

Finn shrugged. "I promise to give you privacy. It's not like I'll be a creeper following you into the bathroom or anything—though it would be hot to see you in the shower..."

I narrowed my eyes at him then laughed.

"I'm joking...sort of. Seriously, though, I'm not sure what will happen when my family gets in their car to go home."

"What do you mean?"

"I haven't been able to leave them. It's like an invisible force has been keeping me with them. Yet I can't do anything to help them. And I don't think my presence is making anything better."

My heart sank at the thought of him being pulled away from me. Losing him so soon after just getting him back would shatter me all over again. "Did the woman say anything about that?"

He closed his eyes and was silent for a minute. "All I'm getting is that I have to stay until it's time and I'll know when that is."

"Does that mean you're psychic now?"

"If I close my eyes and get really quiet, I can hear her again, but I can't predict the future."

"Did anything else change when you died? It's like you sound more grown up."

"I do see things from a different perspective now," he said.

"Wow, I never imagined anything like this could happen to me."

"Ditto. I'm glad it's you."

My heart lit up. "Me, too." My nerves forced me to stand. "Speaking of bathrooms, I could use one."

I didn't have to go, but I didn't want him to see me cry. The bathroom near the theatre was unlocked. Finn pretended to follow me inside, then backed out into the hallway when I waved him away. Once the door was closed, I jumped up and down, holding in a squeal of excitement. I leaned against the wall, letting happy tears fall. He was back, sort of, and I wouldn't let him go this time, if I could help it.

Hearing voices, I wiped my eyes, then flushed the toilet. Glancing at my watch, I realized more than an hour had passed since the start of the memorial. It must be over already.

When I got back outside, he was gone. My heart sank. What if I had imagined the whole thing? I shouldn't have let him out of my sight. Students and teachers were exiting the theatre, their heads down. I froze, willing myself not to fall apart.

Then suddenly he was at my side again.

"Crap! Don't scare me like that! I thought you were gone."

"Oh, right. I promise not to leave without telling you again."

"Better not!"

"So, I know today is Valentine's Day," he said.

"How'd you know that?"

"My dad scribbled "memorial" on our wall calendar, so, anyway, come with me."

I followed him around the corner. He walked through a rose bush and stood behind it. "See this rose?" He pointed to a red rose, its petals still holding tight to each other.

I nodded.

"I want to pick it for you, but I can't." He held his palms up.

"Really?" I asked.

"Yes, really. If I were still *here* here you would've had at least a dozen of these." He walked back toward me. "It's so messed up that I can't even pick this one for you."

I leaned over, careful not to cut myself on the thorns, and bent the stem of the rose he'd chosen for me. "It's the thought that counts, you know, in this case especially."

We sat in my car waiting to see what would happen next. The happiness and hope I'd felt on our first date returned. While not being able to touch him changed so much, being in his presence again was more than enough.

Finn's basketball coach walked his mom, dad, and sister to their black SUV. The coach had been carrying the oversized picture of Finn under his arm, but now handed it to Violet, who pulled it into the backseat with her. The coach hugged Mrs. Peterson and shook Mr. Peterson's hand. His mom wiped her eyes, and his dad's smile looked forced.

I held my breath as their car began to pull away, watching their orange blinker flash while they waited for an opening to turn into the street. I gripped the steering wheel, as if holding onto something would keep Finn with me.

After the car disappeared down the street Finn remained in the seat next to me. I began to breathe again.

"There you have it," he said. "I'm definitely here for you."

CHAPTER 7

The wispy branches of my weeping willow tree hung before us. After a moment of hesitation, I parted the limbs and opened a curtain to the place I could most be myself. The soft clinking of a neighbor's wind chimes floated in the air. I unfolded the blanket that I kept outside and laid it out for us to sit on.

On the drive home, I'd considered why Finn was here and what that meant for me. It was too soon for answers. My stomach churned; all I knew for sure was that I had no control. But I needed some to feel safe.

"Wow." He looked up. Thin rays of sunshine flittered between the skinny branches and right down to the blanket beneath him.

"This is my favorite spot," I said.

He looked at me, "It suits you."

Feeling naked beneath his gaze, I looked down at my hands and gently pulled at a hangnail on my thumb.

"So, should we talk about the elephant in the room?" he asked.

"Which elephant are you referring to?"

"Where my shoes are, of course."

I laughed. Clearly, he was outfitted in the clothes he'd been wearing when he died.

"It's a good thing I fell asleep in my clothes that night, otherwise, I'd just be walking around in my undies." He laughed. "Not that it affects me much, but shoes would complete my ensemble."

"And maybe you could fix your hair a bit?"

His eyes widened and he raised his hands to his head. "Why? Oh, no. Do I have bedhead?"

I nodded, laughing at the hair that stuck up on one side.

"Damn. I don't have a reflection, so I never would've known. Thanks for giving me a complex!"

"It's not like you can control it."

"I'm glad you're not mad at me," he said.

I wanted to squeeze his hand, but we had nothing more than words. "There is nothing to be mad about. If anyone should be mad, maybe it's you."

"Why?" he asked.

"I had a feeling it was all too good to be true, maybe deep inside I knew something was wrong. Maybe I could've prevented...everything."

"That's impossible. There is nothing you could've done."

"And I keep thinking that if I had a time machine I'd go back to that day in kindergarten. I would take your hand and let you help me up."

"You think that would've made a difference?"

"It would've changed the course of our lives, at least with each other."

"You can't put that much weight on one moment," he said. "Besides, we were just kids then."

"Maybe it wouldn't have changed anything, but I'd still like to go back and live that moment differently," I said.

"There are moments I would change too, but it doesn't matter because we can't go back, and I don't think there's much use in wishing we could."

"Aren't you so logical?"

"I think with my head. You think with your heart."

"You think with your heart, too."

"Maybe I do, but also I think dying made me wiser."

"Do you think we were destined to be pulled apart like this?" I asked.

"No way. I'm betting this is part of the reason why I'm here. To give us a little piece of the forever we missed."

Forever. I soaked in his words, and the magic of what we were quickly becoming—an us.

"How long is our forever?" I asked.

"As much as we can cram into the time we have. I'm sorry I don't have specifics, Goodnight—no rulebook, remember?"

"I wish I'd known you were here sooner," I said.

"I had a feeling you were the *her*, but I couldn't get through the force keeping me with my family."

"I wonder why you couldn't come to me right away," I said.

"I've been wondering the same thing. My best guess is that would've been extremely overwhelming to both lose me and get me back at the same time. Too much to handle."

"That makes sense. I'd started thinking about how to let you go. I thought today might've given me some closure," I said.

"Oh," he said.

"I didn't have another choice."

"It would've been the right thing to do. But I'm here now," he said.

"Yes, though I still don't know how this is possible!"

We sat looking at each other, our longing adding to the energetic force between us.

I realized that I'd been so caught up with my feelings that I hadn't thought much about his. "I'm so sorry that you died."

"Thanks," he said. "The dying part didn't hurt, but watching my family find me did. They aren't doing great and there's nothing I can do about it."

"I wish I could help," I said.

"Someday you might be able to. Promise me you will if I ask?"

"Yes, of course." I meant it but wondered what I could possibly do to ease their pain.

"You rock," he said.

"I really don't think I'd be so calm if I'd been the one who died. There is so much more I want to do with my life, like get out of high school and away from Lisa."

"Lisa?" he asked.

"Uh, yeah...my mom."

The sun had begun to set, darkness sinking in on us beneath the willow.

"You call her by her first name?"

"It'll all make sense soon, I'm sure."

He nodded.

"I can't believe my first boyfriend is a ghost." I clapped my hand over my mouth. "Oh, my God. Please forget I said that," I said through my fingers.

"I don't want to forget it. I'm honored." He placed his hand over his heart. "And so, what if I'm a ghost? Let's take what we can get!"

"We don't even know each other—not really." I wondered how love between a living being and a ghost could survive.

"If you think about it, we're just picking up where we left off. We might be fast-tracking a bit, but knowing our time is limited, it's all good, isn't it?"

My blush deepened. Did being a ghost make him this perfect, or was he already perfect?

Yet I wondered if letting him all the way in, allowing him to see things that only Julia had, was safe. "The idea of you being a fly on my wall is freaking me out a little."

"But I'm not a fly on your wall. You can see me, so you'll always know when I'm around. And you can ask me to leave whenever you want."

"I can't ask you to leave. I'm afraid of losing you again."

"I don't think I'll disappear forever if you ask me to leave the room. But if it makes you feel better, I'm happy to spend every single second that I can with you, my alive girlfriend."

I smiled. "Boyfriends usually take their girlfriends on dates."

"Without a body there's not much I can do. I no longer have access to money, and you know I can't change my clothes or brush my hair."

"None of that matters," I said.

"Good." He leaned forward and touched his nose to mine. The prickles of his energy warmed my face.

I couldn't put off letting Finn into my house—into the mess of my life much longer because my stomach was growling. "I need to eat something." I patted my stomach.

"Do you want me to go?" he asked.

"Go? No way! I just feel like I need to warn you about..."

Banging came from inside the house. Finn raised his eyebrows.

"I guess you're about to find out. I just hope this doesn't scare you off."

If I was going to be dating a ghost, there would be no hiding anything from Finn. I stood up and brushed the grass from my pants then folded the blanket and tossed it back onto the lounge chair.

"I know you don't just let anyone in. I've always understood that about you."

"I feel pretty cracked open right now," I said.

My shoulder warmed, as if Finn had given it a squeeze, and I looked down to see his hand there.

As we reached the sliding glass door I saw Lisa in the kitchen, tipping a wine bottle over her nearly full glass. She shook out every drop before tossing the empty container into the recycling bin. The sound of glass against glass made me cringe. It always meant she'd been home a while and the likelihood of her stumbling around with a snarky attitude was high.

I opened the door slowly, preparing to see my home life through Finn's eyes. Lisa's long brown hair streaked with blonde highlights, hung loose and messy at her shoulders. Heavy black mascara and smudged eyeliner framed her eyes. She was slender, but I wouldn't say she was in shape. I'd never seen her exercise, and most of her calories came from alcohol, not from food. She wore a skintight hot-pink sweater over a pair of black dress pants. Her black high-heel shoes toppled lazily against each other on the counter.

She glanced up, then quickly looked away. Lisa never intended to make eye contact with me, and when she did, she'd acted like it was the worst thing in the world.

"I didn't know you were out there." She left the kitchen before I could reply, returning to the blaring sound of a game show on TV in the other room.

Busying myself with dinner prep, I looked in the freezer. Not interested in what I saw there, I looked in the fridge. I pulled out a carton of lettuce, shredded chicken, and ranch dressing. Salad it was.

Lisa never cooked. Mimi had done all the cooking, though she'd never made meals from scratch like Julia's mom. Our meals were comprised of frozen or deli items and whatever came from cans and jars, but they were home cooked. I hadn't realized it at the time, but in preparation for her death Mimi had taught me the basics, knowing Lisa wouldn't be stepping up her cooking game after she was gone.

Breaking the silence, Finn asked, "So...that was Lisa?"

I looked up at him, finally allowing myself to gauge his reaction to what he'd witnessed. From what I could tell, his mom was the opposite of Lisa.

"Super motherly, right?" I waved my hand in the direction she'd gone, pretending to hold a wineglass in my other hand.

"She's young," he said.

"She was only nineteen when she had me," I said. How old she'd been when I was born had never been something we'd discussed but I'd sleuthed. When Julia and I were about ten we'd snuck into Lisa's purse to look at her driver's license. Then we did the math.

"Wow," Finn said.

"Mimi raised me, until she died when I was twelve. This is her house."

"How did she die?" he said.

"Cancer. She knew for a while that she was sick and never told me, at least not until it was too late. I've never really forgiven her for that."

Considering Finn couldn't go anywhere, me being just as transparent as he literally was seemed unavoidable, but still, I was surprised how much I had already let Finn in under my turtle shell—into my inner thoughts.

It was too much. I changed the subject, "Anyway, just don't tell me you think Lisa's hot."

"God, Goodnight, I'd never refer to your mom as hot. She looks tired and..." He paused before adding, "Lost."

I shrugged, having stopped looking at her in any meaningful way years ago. "Maybe she is, but it's whatever really. We pretty much just ignore each other."

"That sucks," Finn said.

"It is what it is."

"Where's your grandpa?"

"He died, too, when I was about three or four. Heart attack. I don't have many memories of him."

"And your dad?" He asked, lightly, somehow aware it might be a touchy subject.

I shrugged. "I have no idea. I've never met him. I honestly don't even know if he exists..."

"Oh, that's a lot, Goodnight," he said.

A lot.

I sighed, then tossed my ingredients into a bowl, grabbed a fork, and sat next to him.

"You didn't have much chance to be a kid, huh?"

No one had ever stated that so directly before. Julia and I had always glossed over the topic, though I knew she felt the same way. "Not really."

"You and Lisa are just like roommates?" he asked.

"Yeah. Thinking about it that way makes me feel better when she brings loser 'boyfriends' home."

Finn shook his head. "Did she bring guys here when your Mimi was still around?"

"No. Then she'd just stay gone for days at a time and come home hung over. She never drank in front of Mimi. After Mimi died, Lisa stopped trying to cover up what she was doing. Which made it obvious it wasn't me she'd been trying to shield her problems from."

I knew from the Morgans that my family wasn't typical. Julia had a mom, dad and brothers who acted how it seemed a family should. To an outsider, my home life wouldn't make sense and it'd never made much sense to me either.

Finn's family wasn't a shattered mess like mine. They were a perfect happy unit—until now—because now they didn't have him.

"I wish I could eat with you. Really be with you. I'm missing so much."

A breeze grazed my neck, as if he'd lifted my hair, but it still hung there, motionless.

"You're just too good to be true, aren't you, Mr. Finn Peterson?"

"Is it even possible to be too good to be true and dead at the same time?" He raised his eyebrows at me.

"Yes. We take what we can get, right?" I sighed, wishing I could lean into him.

This wasn't a rom-com. Walking hand in hand toward the sunset was just the final scene of a book or movie. We never found out what happened to the characters when the sun came up the next day and real life began. This was our next day, our real life. Being together like this was magical, and yet, I knew a real happily ever after ending didn't exist for us.

I looked up, realizing I'd been drifting in my thoughts for several minutes. "You're sure you can't hear what I'm thinking?"

"If only. Then I'd have Claire on the brain all the time," he said.

"That's cheesy." I laughed. Hearing him say my first name spread warmth through me. I'd take our happy ending in moments like these and make them into forever.

"What's cheesy?" Lisa asked from the doorway.

I jumped at the sound of her voice and her sudden presence in the kitchen. "Oh, I was just thinking about something somebody said at school."

I'd have to pay more attention to my surroundings—if I was caught too many times talking to an empty room, it would raise questions I didn't want to answer.

"O-k-a-y."

Lisa opened a cabinet and pulled out another wine bottle. She twisted the cap and dropped it into the trash. Leaning slightly, she left with the full container.

"It sort of makes sense now," Finn said.

"What does?" I asked, shoving a fork full of salad into my mouth.

"Why you are the way you are. I never really thought about kids being affected by their parents, but of course it would make a huge difference in who we become."

"It's not something you think about unless you have crappy parents," I said.

Finn nodded. "I guess I was lucky and didn't know it."

"You were."

"I'm worried about Vi. She won't have the same loving and together parents anymore."

"No, she won't." I remembered the blank look on his mom's face at the memorial. Finn had described Lisa's look as lost; I would use the same word for his mom's.

Finn took a walk while I got ready for bed. Once he was gone, I sent Julia a text message apologizing for not messaging her sooner. I hated putting her off, but if I FaceTimed her tonight, she'd know something was up. The hollow gaze of the last two weeks had been replaced with delight and the sudden change wouldn't make sense to her without knowing the truth. I couldn't prove his existence over the phone—and besides, if I told her about Finn, he wouldn't be mine alone anymore.

Finn yelped from outside. I peered out the window and watched him land on the grass in my front yard. I wondered what other crazy things he'd been trying in his new form. He was literally unbreakable now.

He would be the first boy in my room. It was mostly free from clutter, and my dirty clothes were in the hamper. Even in my grief, I'd kept it clean. Mimi had wanted me to wake up fresh, carrying nothing over from the previous day. She'd molded me in a way she hadn't been able to mold Lisa and I'd let her.

I straightened some of the books on my bookcase then picked up the framed picture of me and Mimi. It was a selfie she'd taken of us one day after we'd been gardening. Her brownish gray hair was covered with a floppy hat, and she had dirt on her chin. I wore sunglasses and a toothy grin.

"You'd never believe this, Mimi." I traced a finger around her side of the photo. "Or maybe you would."

I pulled open the window and called out lightly. "Finn, you can come up now."

When he appeared seconds later, I screamed. I'd been expecting him to use the front door, but of course, he had no need for that. Lisa was passed out on the couch, so I didn't worry about her hearing me.

"Time for bed?" he asked.

"For me." I hunched my shoulders, uncomfortable wearing pajamas in front of him. "Feel free to go and do whatever ghostly things you need to do while I sleep."

"I can't go far. I tried to run down the street and hit the same invisible wall that kept me from leaving my family."

"Sort of like a restraining order in reverse?"

"Something like that, but I don't feel restrained." He grinned.

I wondered how many times he could melt my heart before I got used to it. "So, I guess you're really stuck with me."

"Stuck is not the way I see it." Then he asked, "Whatcha looking at?"

I hadn't realized I was still holding the frame in my hand. I turned it around.

Finn bent over and peered at it. "You look happy. Wait, who is that with you?" He moved closer, his face only inches away.

"It's Mimi."

"No way," he said.

"What?"

"She's so familiar."

"I'm sure you saw her at school over the years," I said.

His brows furrowed and he sat down on the bed.

I placed the frame back on my desk. "What's going on?"

"It's beginning to make more sense now."

"Not to me."

He looked up at me. "She was the woman in the light. After I died. It was her."

My heart rate sped up and I dropped onto the bed too. Mimi smiled at me from inside the frame.

"She sent me back to you."

Electricity sparked on my fingers. I looked down to see Finn's hand on mine.

"Are you okay?"

"You're sure it was her?" I asked.

"Positive."

"Did she say anything about me?"

"She never specifically said your name..."

"So, there was no message for me?"

"Not that I recall. But she said so much, I could've missed it."

If she had the power to send Finn back to me, why wouldn't she have sent words for me with him? I looked at her photo then at Finn. Unless he was the message—and sending him back to me was a gift.

"What's happening in that head of yours?"

"What isn't? This day is insane," I said.

He sighed. "I shouldn't expect you to be able to just accept all of this otherworldly stuff."

"Do you think Mimi sent you back to me?"

"Since you are the *her*, and that woman in the picture is the woman I saw, then yes, it definitely seems that way."

Had Finn not been standing before me as a ghost, I wouldn't have thought it possible that Mimi could be trying to reconnect with me after all this time, but it was practically undeniable.

"This is wild. My heart is happy, but my mind is overwhelmed," I said.

"I'm happy about your heart," he smiled. "Maybe sleep will help with your mind."

I nodded.

"Which side of the bed do you sleep on?"

The thought of Finn sleeping next to me was exhilarating and scary.

"Too soon?" He smiled.

Our time was limited and shouldn't be wasted. My heart responded for me. "Nope."

I turned off the light and lay down on the right side of the bed. Finn lay down facing me.

"I really wish I could kiss you." His voice was gruff with wanting.

"Me, too."

He shifted toward me. "And hold you."

My body ached for his touch. Finn moved so close I had to refocus my eyes to see him—otherwise I'd be looking through to the wall behind him.

We pressed into each other. My lips, moist with Chapstick, touched his ghostly lips, sending a sweet shock through me. He wrapped his ghostly presence around my physical form, and I lit up everywhere.

"It's not the same, is it?"

"Don't let go."

He didn't.

I cozied myself up in him and the blankets. Sleep had been inconsistent since he'd died, but now my body relaxed against what was left of him. Afraid he wouldn't be there when I woke up, I tried to push sleep away.

As if Finn heard my thoughts, he said, "I'm not going anywhere."

I believed him and let sleep come.

CHAPTER 8

Since Finn's death, the short time between dreaming and waking was the only place he wasn't gone. Each morning, after memory returned, the crashing waves of grief hit me again, tangling around me like seaweed.

Not ready to see yet if yesterday had only been a dream, I turned off my alarm without opening my eyes, held my breath and waited.

"I'm still here," he whispered in my ear.

Breathing out, I wondered if the fear of being left would ever go away.

I allowed my eyelids to flutter open. Not only was he still with me, but I knew he wanted to be.

"Thank God," I said.

"You're beautiful," he said.

My face flushed. "Even like this?"

"Especially like this. Watching you sleep is one of my new favorite things."

"I would kiss you so hard right now if I could," I said.

We held our lips close. My heart hummed.

"Did you know you hold your hands together when you sleep?" he asked.

I sat up and pulled my tangled hair back with the black hairband around my wrist. "I do?"

"It's adorable."

"That's odd. I hope I didn't snore or drool."

He laughed. "No. There may have been the occasional fart, but that's no biggie," he said. "I can't smell!"

I covered my face with my hands. "How embarrassing!"

He smiled. "Don't be embarrassed—just be glad you can fart."

My first day back at Palm Row Pizza turned out to be my first full day with Finn's ghost. Just out of view from the glass double doors, I leaned against a cement pillar, clutching my hat and freshly washed apron.

"This is going to be weird," I said.

"Can I help make it less weird?"

"I doubt it. Tyler knows how sad I've been. Now that you're here…he'll notice a difference in me. I'm not sure how to act now."

"There's that name Tyler again. I'm picturing a balding old man with a beer belly. Please tell me I'm wrong."

I laughed. "He's twenty and doesn't have a beer belly. He was a couple years ahead of us in school."

"Hmm."

"I can't tell him I can see your ghost."

"Do you think he'd believe you if you did?"

I shrugged. "I don't want to share you, but I'm not a good liar. Good or bad, my emotions are all over my face."

Weekends were busy and when I walked in, Tyler and several other employees were on the phones behind the counter. The mumble of words and dishes being washed in the back was an abrupt difference from the calm outside. I kept my head down but felt Tyler's eyes on me as I opened the door to the back.

After putting my things in a locker, I clocked in. Then glanced at the schedule as I pulled my ponytail through the hole in my hat.

"Just so you know, you look super-hot right now." Finn had a serious look on his face.

I smiled. The boy must really like me if he thought I looked good in my uniform.

"I'm going to check this place out." He turned to explore, walking through racks of dishes as he went.

"Hey," Tyler said from behind me. Startled, I jumped.

Prior to turning to face him, I forced my smile down. He was closer than I'd expected, I backed away, bumping into the wall. Out of obligation to Finn, creating space between Tyler and me seemed like the right thing to do.

"Are you okay?" He reached his hand out to my forearm. His eyes narrowed and drilled into mine.

"I'm feeling better every day," I said.

"Are you clocked in yet, Claire?" Robby called out from the cook table.

Grateful for a reason to walk away from Tyler, I rushed to help Robby.

Finn popped his head through the glass window of the walk-in freezer, yelling, "Hello, Goodnight!" Rolling my eyes at him, I attempted to hide my smile.

My smart watch blew up with texts from Julia. I read them as they flashed on the small screen.

JULIA: *C!*

JULIA: *Are you okay?*

JULIA: *Call me!*

The last time I talked to Julia I'd been a sad mess. I pushed away the thoughts of what I would tell her and focused on what was in front of me.

Hours passed and occasionally Finn rushed up behind me, trying to make me laugh. He pretended to kick Robby in the butt and waved his hand through the bill of his hat. Robby reacted when his hat was touched and asked if I'd felt a breeze in the room. Holding in my giggles, I shook my head and continued to work.

After a while of Finn hanging out near me, I motioned for him to go outside. Unable to acknowledge that he was there was difficult, and I worried about him being bored.

"How are you two doing back there?" Tyler called from the front of the store.

"We could use some help stocking the table when someone gets a minute!" I called back after scanning our ingredients.

Tyler appeared next to me. "What do you need?"

"Cheese, jalapeños, olives, and pineapple."

"You got it." Tyler rushed to the freezer and returned with a twenty-five-pound box of cheese. He tore the clear tape off the cardboard, opened the plastic bag, then quickly tipped it over, dumping the white strands of mozzarella into the large bin. He glanced at me as he pulled out the cans and opened them up with the industrial size opener and filled up the containers. When he walked away, the table was fully stocked.

Things slowed down by the end of my shift. While I waited for orders, I folded pizza boxes. It was a soothing and satisfying task to fill the empty chrome wire shelving up with ready to use boxes. The dry smell of cardboard, a mix of dust and paper, filtered through the air.

I hadn't seen Finn in over an hour. The quiet gave me time to process. I texted Julia to let her know I'd call her when my shift was over.

Tyler came to the back of the store and washed his hands in the small porcelain sink. He took off his hat and ran his fingers through his hair, shaking off his hat head. He raised his arms in the air, stretched, and moaned, then twisted his midsection back and forth until his back cracked, a bit of his muscular stomach showed, and I looked away.

"How has today been for you?" He leaned against the delivery rack.

"Busy." I tossed a box onto the growing stack.

He raised his eyebrows.

"It has been!" I said.

"How was the memorial?"

"It wasn't exactly the closure I'd expected."

"You seem better though," he said.

"I am." I busied myself with my task.

"You know I'm always here if you need to talk."

"I know, thank you. I appreciate everything you've done."

"Right. Yeah, cool." He looked at his feet, then back up at me. "Oh, hey, Sonya is sick. Do you want her 4:00 to 8:00 shift tomorrow night?"

"I can't tomorrow."

"Really?"

"Yeah, there's this school project I have to work on." The lie came out more easily than I'd expected or wanted.

"Homework has never stopped you from taking shifts before, but okay. I'll find someone else. Did you want to grab something to eat after your shift? I'm off, but I can wait for you."

I'd forgotten all about our usual Sunday night dinner.

"Nah, I was just going to take home a pizza tonight."

He tried to hide the flash of hurt on his face by turning away, but I saw it. Under normal circumstances, I would've caved and gone to dinner with him, but not now, with Finn waiting for me.

"Got it. Well, have a good night." He pulled his keys from his pocket and jangled them in his hand.

My stomach tightened as the door shut behind him, a part of us closing with it. I knew that I'd hurt him in a way I didn't quite want to understand. It wasn't until the door had fully closed that I saw Finn standing there.

"Tyler?" Finn asked.

I nodded.

"You can go to dinner with him, Goodnight," he said.

I glanced around the room. A few drivers were laughing and talking while washing pans in the large sinks. They were out of earshot.

Trying to shake the Tyler encounter off, I said, "No, I can't. You're my priority. What have you been up to?"

"I can't get too far from you, but the usual, walking through walls, jumping off buildings, and being a fly on the wall. People have the most interesting conversations. I feel guilty listening in."

"I'm glad you're back."

"I seriously hate to say this, but I can tell that dude cares about you."

"He's just my friend," I said.

"Maybe to you, but you're more than just a friend to him."

I'd been pushing away this knowing since shortly after Julia moved away and I certainly didn't want to face it now. Grateful to hear a new order print, I rushed to make the pizzas since that saved me from answering Finn.

Outside, after work, the air was cool and clean. The rows of palm trees stood still and well-postured, like guards against the light of the moon.

My phone buzzed in my purse. A picture of my beautiful best friend flashed on the screen. I couldn't ignore her forever, so I picked up.

"C! You're majorly turtling!"

"I'm sorry, J. It's been crazy," I said.

"What has?"

"Yesterday was…an emotional day. I didn't feel much like talking."

She was silent a beat. "Well, you should've called to say you didn't want to talk." I imagined her standing with a hand on her hip.

"That would've involved talking," I said.

"Boo!" Finn jumped out from behind me.

I leapt into the air. "You've got to be kidding me!" I swatted at him.

"What happened?" Julia asked.

"Oh! Um, it was just Tyler. He snuck up behind me. Hold on a second." I clicked the mute button.

Finn laughed. "Sorry, I didn't realize you were on the phone."

I shook my head, trying not to laugh too. "That was way too cliché, Finn. Come on, you can't be the ghost that yells 'Boo'!"

He held his hands up in defense, smiling. "You know I had to do it at least once."

I waved the phone in my hand. "It's Julia. What do you think? Should I tell her about you?"

"It's up to you," Finn said.

"Can't you just make this decision for me?"

"You know her better than I do. Besides, you're the one concerned with people thinking you're crazy…"

"Which is a legitimate concern! Are you telling me you want to spend the rest of whatever time we have left with me locked up in a psych ward?"

"You're right. You still have a life to think about."

I clicked unmute. "I'm back."

"What happened?"

"Tyler wanted to know if I could pick up a shift tomorrow."

"Cool, let me say hello to him," she said.

"Oh, sorry, he's already gone."

"You aren't getting dinner?"

"Not tonight," I said.

She muttered something I didn't understand.

I changed the subject. "How's Oregon?"

"Rainy and still not California." She sighed.

"What'd you do this weekend?"

"Movies with the fam bam," she said.

I picked up the pizza box that I'd set on the ground when she called and motioned Finn to walk to the car with me. "Sounds fun." The hole inside me ached for the Morgans.

"I miss you," Julia said.

"I miss you too, J." I unlocked the car.

We said our goodbyes and I turned to Finn. "Did you want to drive by and check on your family?"

"It's okay, you've had a long day at the office." He smiled. "Let's go home."

CHAPTER 9

Finn leaned forward when I pulled into my driveway. "What the hell?"

I recognized his dad's SUV parked against the curb in front of my house. Finn flew through the windshield.

I wanted to stop time, to undo what Finn was likely to witness. There was a common theme among the men Lisa brought home. They all ended up in her bed.

After parking in the garage, I crept low to where Finn stood outside the living room window. Through the white gauzy curtain, I saw Finn's dad sitting stiffly on the edge of the couch. Lisa's feet were tucked beneath her, a wine glass in her hand.

"Why is he here?" Finn asked. His face had shrunk up and he looked like a younger version of himself, confused.

Unable to put my arms around him, I reached out. My hand passed straight through.

Pulling back, I asked, "Do you think he could be here to see me?"

"Hmm. I didn't think about that. I just assumed…"

"That he would be sleeping with her because that's what she does?"

He nodded, his ghost eyes wide.

"I don't blame you. What do you want me to do?" I asked.

Finn ignored me and floated inside. He didn't know how lucky he was to find his dad fully clothed and in an upright position.

I'd lost my appetite but carried my pizza into the kitchen from the garage anyway. I announced my presence by slamming the door shut behind me.

When I turned the corner to the living room Lisa's back straightened, a surprised expression on her face. "Oh! Claire," she said.

She'd never been fazed by the fact that I saw her with men. Her usual mode of operation was to ignore me, and her men followed suit. I've always assumed she told them I was her little sister and I doubt they ever cared to question her.

Finn's dad, however, stood up when he saw me.

Lisa unfolded her legs. "You usually aren't home from work this soon on Sundays."

Finn stood face to face with his dad, his eyebrows furrowed.

Lisa had never expressed interest in my comings and goings, so it was odd that she was aware of my routine. I planted my feet firmly on the carpet and shrugged.

When she realized that I wasn't going to run away like I usually did, she spoke. "Eric, this is Claire..."

I held my breath, wondering if she'd introduce me as her daughter.

She paused for a moment, then added, "Claire, this is Eric."

Eric approached me, holding his hand out. Finn quickly moved out of his way. Eric's large man hand enfolded mine in a clammy, yet strong handshake. He clearly didn't remember me from the basketball game.

Having never looked so directly at Finn's dad before, I hadn't been aware of their similarities. Now, up close, I caught a glimpse of what Finn would've looked like had he lived into his forties. His dad was handsome, even with the sadness sagging beneath his eyes.

I tried to imagine Lisa meeting this broken man at a bar. Unable to see Eric picking up women in his grieving state, my mind argued over who would've approached whom, and what led him here.

Finn paced the room, muttering under his breath.

I told Eric, "I know...knew your son."

Eric's eyes turned glassy, and he slumped back down on the couch. After releasing a heavy sigh, he asked, "Do you go to Palm Row High?"

I nodded. "We've met. You might know me as Goodnight?"

He rubbed one of his eyes, then said, "Oh, God, yes. Of course, I know who you are. I'm sorry I didn't recognize you. Clearly, I'm not myself lately."

Finn moved next to me. "You can say that again. Please find out why he's here."

Unable to explain the obvious to Finn, I kept my eyes on his dad. Anyone else would've been in Lisa's bedroom by now. Perhaps he hadn't intended to cheat on Finn's mom.

Eric studied his hands. Had I been in a similarly grieved state, without Finn as a ghost at my side, I would've handled this situation quite differently. I would've offered my condolences and would've wanted to talk to him about his son. However, in this case, my allegiance was to my ghost boyfriend. I needed to find a way to get his dad home to his family, so I went straight for the jugular.

"I thought maybe you were here about Finn. I wasn't aware you knew..." I motioned toward Lisa.

His eyes shifted away from me, and he twisted the thick gold wedding band on his finger.

"Who is Finn?" Lisa asked.

"My son. He passed away recently. Very unexpectedly. I wanted to forget for just a moment." His eyes found mine, as if wanting me, not Lisa, to understand why he was there with someone other than his wife.

"Oh," Lisa said. "I'm very sorry for your loss."

My mouth threatened to drop open, surprised by her unexpected empathy, but I clenched my jaw instead.

Eric stood up. Finn shifted sideways then lunged through him. Eric staggered back against the wall. He stayed there, leaning against it, tears slipping down his cheeks, then he sank to the floor. In seconds Lisa was there, wrapping her arms around him. Eric muttered Finn's name.

His sorrow filled the room. Finn's ghost was only a temporary Band-Aid over the hole in my heart. I knew he couldn't stay with me forever, and when he left, my wound would be exposed once again. Yet, even in my own heartache, I knew that the depth of my loss was nothing compared to the loss of a son.

Finn stood over Lisa and his dad, bent together. I wanted to pull them apart for him, to break their strange connection. He reached down to touch his father's head but then stopped himself.

"I can't watch this, Goodnight. I have to go." He vanished through the wall into the backyard.

The tension in my jaw released and my mouth dropped open. Lisa was comforting a stranger in a way she'd never done with me. Whispering, "Everything will be okay," and "I'm here," as she ran her hand up and down his back.

I left them there to search for Finn.

I peered outside, pressing my forehead against the cold glass of the sliding door, a buffer against the night. Once in the backyard, I walked to my tree. Seconds after I'd brushed the branches aside, Finn's energy burst out from the shadows.

Not being able to embrace him was an ache I felt deep in my bones. "I'm sorry, Finn," I said.

"I can't go back in there."

"We don't have to," I said.

"What does this mean for my family?"

"This definitely doesn't look good, but nothing has happened between them, yet."

Finn sighed. "But he shouldn't even be here."

I nodded. "You're right. It doesn't make sense. I saw your parents together at the basketball game. They clearly love each other."

"He's going to ruin everything! And just so he can forget for one night?"

We stayed outside. After a while, I wrapped myself up in the blanket I'd always kept beneath my tree. Singing crickets and ticking sprinklers from the neighbor's house played their nightly song. Without saying it, we both knew we were waiting for the sound of Eric's car starting up, but it never came.

Finn told me stories of his parents, how they'd held hands whenever they walked together, kissed hello and goodbye, and how they'd laughed—deep belly laughs—all the time. He pondered over how quickly they'd fallen away from each other.

After he'd talked himself out, he recommended I go to sleep. Looking up at him, I lay back on the lawn chair. He pressed his lips against my forehead with the best kind of kiss he could manage as a ghost. I closed my eyes. My cheeks burned warm beneath a gaze that I knew hadn't yet shifted away from me.

Had it been me looking down at him, I would've etched his face into my memory; the way his lips turned down, how his eyelashes looked resting on his skin, the serenity of approaching sleep.

When I woke up, I was alone. My phone, pulled from my back pocket, informed me that it was 2:33 a.m.

I stepped out from my tree. "Finn?" I whispered.

He didn't reply. Silence filled the night. Even the crickets were sleeping now. It was just me, and a sliver of the moon amongst a sky sprinkled with stars.

The need to pee and my desire to find Finn led me inside the house. The first floor was quiet. My pizza box sat soggy and untouched on the counter. Two empty wine glasses remained on the coffee table, so close they were almost touching.

"Finn?" I whispered again.

"I'm here." He appeared from upstairs.

"What are you doing?" I scratched my head, groggily.

"Checking up on my dad," Finn said.

I glanced toward his dad's car, out of place on a street that wasn't his.

"Did you go into Lisa's room?"

Finn's eyes shifted to the ceiling then back to me so quickly I almost missed it.

"What's wrong?" I asked.

"Nothing. They're, uh…sleeping."

"Did they…?"

"I don't think so," Finn said.

I knew his dad wasn't like the others. "That's good news."

"But he's still here. He shouldn't be here. Anyway, it's late, Goodnight. I shouldn't have asked you to stay outside. You should sleep in your own bed."

"I've slept out there plenty of times, but my bed does sound good," I said.

Finn followed me upstairs. In the bathroom, I quickly sat on the toilet. The door was slightly ajar. It was a strangely intimate moment, knowing he could hear me peeing.

I kicked off my shoes and changed into pajamas in my closet. Finally, snug in my blankets and Finn, I closed my eyes again. I could've sworn I heard mumbling voices before I drifted off.

The next morning, after I showered and got ready for school, Finn and I went downstairs. Lisa and Eric were at the kitchen table with steaming cups of coffee in front of them. Lisa's laptop was open, and they both looked away from the screen when I entered.

"Morning," Lisa said.

I paused mid-step and glanced over at her, my eyebrows raised. Lisa kept her eyes trained on me, waiting for a response.

Unfamiliar with us greeting each other this way, I mumbled back.

"Good morning, Claire." Eric stood up. "I want to apologize for last night. I shouldn't have fallen apart like that." He looked away from me.

"I get it. Losing Finn is a really big deal."

He rubbed his hands against his unshaven cheeks then turned to Lisa. "Good luck." He motioned to her computer.

"Thank you. I appreciate everything," Lisa said.

"No problem and I appreciate the...advice." He cleared his throat. "So, I guess, maybe, I'll see you around?" His words hung in the air and weren't addressed to anyone in particular.

Finn followed him outside.

I filled a coffee mug a third of the way, added vanilla creamer, and stirred until the liquid spun into a creamy light brown.

"How did you know Finn?" Lisa asked.

I froze with the coffee cup halfway to my mouth. Hot liquid swished and slightly spilled over onto my fingers. I set the mug down and licked the coffee away. "We've gone to the same school since kindergarten."

"Oh. I had no idea you knew him so well," she said.

I turned to face her. "How would you have known?"

Lisa pulled her body back in response to my tone. "Right, I don't know, but I'm sorry you lost your friend."

"Not that you'd care, but he was more than a friend. Did you sleep with Mr. Peterson?"

I had never once questioned her about what she did or with whom. She glared at me. "That's none of your business."

"In this case, it is, and he's married and grieving. You took advantage of that."

Her eyes narrowed. "You don't know anything about it, and I don't have to explain myself to you."

She picked up her computer and walked out of the room.

"Find someone else to play with," I called out behind her. My face was hot, and my fists clenched at my side. My legs itched to run, to get away from her and the house.

"What happened?" Finn asked, suddenly beside me.

"She won't tell me what happened."

"It's okay," Finn said.

"It's not."

"We're going to fix things," Finn said. "We can start with checking on Violet."

At school, we looked for Violet in places Finn said she typically hung out, but she wasn't in any of them. He was confused about why she hadn't returned to school yet.

After school was over, we drove to his house to look for her there. When we pulled up, he pointed out the overgrown grass, the weeds in his mom's garden, and the trash bins at the end of the driveway on a non-trash day.

"It's the same as it was when I left them," he said.

"It's only been a few weeks." I remembered how my normal routines had lapsed after Mimi died. Surviving without her had consumed all my energy and nothing else seemed important anymore.

"I guess so," he said.

"We're not doing this ghost whisperer style, are we?" I asked.

"Nah. At least not yet," Finn said. "Wait for me here."

Ten minutes after he'd gone inside, Violet rushed out the front door and hopped on a bike leaning against the side of the house. I ducked down and put my hand over my face. She took off, pedaling down the street, wiping tears from her eyes. A moment later Finn was back in the car with me.

"Is everything okay?" I asked.

He shrugged. "Not really. Care for a trip to the mall?"

I turned the keys. "Is that where Violet is going?"

"I think so. You know the little cafe at the east side of the mall?"

I nodded.

"We can wait for her there."

"Got it." I began driving. "How was your mom?"

"The same? The house is a mess. There are dirty dishes all over the kitchen. It's not like my mom. She's such a neat freak."

"Cleaning up won't bring her son back," I said.

He nodded. "She was in my room, lying on my bed. I touched her and she felt my presence. I shouldn't have done it. I only made things worse."

"It's because they can't see you. What happened with Violet?"

"She walked in and heard my mom whispering my name. Violet yelled that I was gone, then quickly apologized, but Mom just started crying again. That's when Violet rushed off."

"This has to be so hard for them," I said.

"Before I walked out, I said goodbye to my mom. I can't keep going back there. It's like I'm haunting them." He banged his hand through the dashboard, groaning in frustration at the lack of impact.

"You aren't haunting them in a scary way. Besides, what choice have you had?"

"You're right, I didn't choose this. But I do need to help them find a way to move on."

"Maybe she'll be able to let go more easily when she can't feel you anymore." After Mimi died her presence was everywhere, but in time I felt her less and less and a life without her emerged.

"I guess even in death it's possible to overstay your welcome." He clenched his hands into fists. "This is so frustrating, Goodnight. What am I really doing here if I can't help? And where are all the other ghosts? I can't be the only one, can I?"

"Maybe you can only see what you're meant to see, like the rest of us."

"But why can you see me, really?"

"You're here due to the magic of Mimi, right?" I asked.

Finn rested his hand on my leg, his energy radiated through my jeans. "Yes, but I feel like I'm failing them."

"Well, you have helped me in more ways than you could understand," I said.

"I'd be irrelevant without you."

"Would it be weird if I said the same thing about you?" I asked.

He placed his hand on mine and smiled. We drove the rest of the way in silence.

CHAPTER 10

We sat at a table, on the outskirts of the cafe. A group of college kids sat talking and laughing. Their textbooks lay open before them, unread.

I reached into my purse, pulled out my earbuds, and pushed one of them into my ear. If someone saw me talking, they would assume I was on the phone.

"Smart."

"Just in case," I said.

"I'd buy you a coffee, if I could." He reviewed the menu.

"If only we could be a normal coffee-drinking couple," I said.

Finn nodded, then stood up when he saw Violet approaching. "She's alone. Good. I was hoping you could talk to her." He glanced down at me.

Sweat moistened my palms. "OMG, thanks for the heads-up! What do you want me to say?"

"Just be yourself," he said.

I rolled my eyes at him. Being myself was only something I could do after knowing someone. Finn waved me forward. I forced myself to move into line behind Violet.

Her brown hair hung longer than mine, the ends dyed a deep purple. The frames of her glasses matched the purple in her hair. She was tall like Finn and had several inches on me.

"She'll talk to you. Just get her attention."

I faked a sneeze. Finn gave me a thumbs up.

Violet immediately turned around. "Bless you." Then her red-rimmed eyes widened behind her glasses. "Goodnight! Uh, I mean Claire. Hi."

I shrugged. "I liked it when your brother called me Goodnight."

Her eyes lit up. "You know I'm Finn's sister?"

"Of course I do. I'm so sorry he's gone," I said.

"Thank you. Me, too." She glanced at her place in line, then turned back to me. "Would you mind if I sat with you? Or are you here with someone?" She looked around the cafe and straight through Finn.

Finn touched my arm and my pulse raced. "Let her know you'll buy her drink. I'll tell you what to order."

"Yes, I'm alone, and yes, of course you can join me. Why don't you go grab some seats and I'll get you a drink?"

"Sure." She smiled and pushed her glasses up on her nose, before stepping out of line.

Finn helped me place her order, then went to join his sister while I waited for the order.

I set the vanilla bean Frappuccinos with whipped cream and caramel drizzle, in front of Violet.

"What's this?"

"It's a..."

"It's Finn's drink. Whenever he brought me coffee, this is what he bought both of us."

I was at a loss for words, as I'd assumed Finn had me order her typical drink. Finn smiled beside me. If only I could punch his arm.

"You ordered the same thing for yourself?" she asked.

"It's not something I normally get, but I figured I'd try it. Strange coincidence that this was Finn's drink," I mumbled.

We awkwardly sipped our drinks for a moment.

"Well, what do you think?" she asked.

"It's delicious," I said.

"Finn's favorite. I wish…Anyway, I'm glad we ran into each other. I haven't been back to school yet, but I've been hoping to talk to you."

"You have?"

"Yeah." She lifted the lid off her cup and stirred her drink with the straw. "I know you went out with Finn before he…died."

Finn watched our interaction like he was watching a tennis game.

Talking about Finn would make this conversation easy. I'd never had a problem with that. "Yes, and it was amazing. Thank you for helping him set up the date," I said.

"Totally. He was mad lovesick for you!" Her eyes shone, both happy and sad.

"Mad lovesick? Is that a thing?" Finn laughed.

I stopped myself from swatting his arm.

"Was he?" I tried to sound surprised and pleased at the same time.

"He actually asked me for advice. A few days before…you know. He came into my room and said he didn't love Kelly and never had. Then he told me about a girl he'd always liked but didn't know very well. He asked me what he should do. Obviously, I told him to follow his heart!"

I sat, unmoving, wanting to soak up her words as if Finn wasn't beside me. Had he not returned to me, my broken parts would've needed to hear this. An overwhelming sense of warmth wrapped around me, goosebumps pricked my skin and tears gathered in the corners of my eyes.

She watched me, her eyes beginning to water too.

The pain of briefly having him—of hoping for a future that was ripped out from under me—came rushing back. Had I not been able to see Finn, I wondered if her words would've had the power to ease my grief and provide me with a somewhat happy ending to our story. As if his feelings for me, told through his sister, could've been a magical, golden glue squeezed along the cracks of my heart, a salve with the power to pull the pieces back together.

"Him being gone after that must've been so hard for you." She pulled out a napkin from the dispenser for me.

"Heartbreaking," I said. "But it couldn't have been anything compared to how you feel."

"Everything feels wrong without him here."

"It does." I placed my hand over hers, hoping to comfort her in a way that my words never could.

"This might sound odd, but I wanted to thank you." She turned her hand over, so she was holding mine.

"For what?"

"I've thought about Finn's last few days a million times. I realized that he probably died happy because of you. And I think he'd want you to know that. So, I wanted you to know that."

"She's right." Finn put his hand over mine that still clutched Violet's.

Violet and Finn both looked at me, love sparkling in their gazes. I put my other hand over my heart, willing the healing to sink in and stay long after Finn was gone again.

"This is everything to me, Violet. He means...or...meant so much to me."

"It makes me so happy to hear you say that. Wherever Finn is, I'm sure he's doing his 'I just scored a basket' happy dance." She looked up toward the ceiling like he was up there somewhere.

"She's right, again!" Finn stood up and swayed back and forth, his body a rolling wave with his arms stretched high in the air.

"I'm sure he is." I laughed softly, wishing she could see him too.

"Do you think he knew how you felt about him?" Violet asked.

"Absolutely," I said.

In her smile, I saw both Finn and their dad in her expression. "How is your family holding up?" I asked, recognizing the absurdity of the question after it left my lips. However, there was never a good way to ask about how grieving people were.

"Mom is a zombie. Dad is working a lot. He didn't come home last night. I don't think my mom noticed or even cared. I just keep waiting for things to be normal again. But I know they can't be." Her bottom lip trembled.

"I'm sorry, Violet. We don't have to talk about this if you don't want to." I held a napkin out for her, as she'd done for me.

She accepted my offering and wiped her eyes beneath her glasses. "It's okay. I don't have anyone to talk to. At least no one who seems to get it. My mom hasn't accepted that he's gone, and my dad is super frustrated with her. I am too, I guess."

I squeezed her hand again and looked into her eyes, hoping she saw understanding there. "That's hard."

"I don't want to be locked in sadness forever like my mom seems to be. Finn would be so upset to see us like this. He would want us to find some happiness again."

My heart warmed, knowing that Finn wanted exactly that, and Violet got it.

"I agree," I said. "You need support, though, Violet. Can you talk to your friends?"

"Like I said, they don't get it. The school called and left a message saying I could talk to the school counselor, but I haven't been back yet. Finn is the only person I want to talk to—you know?"

I nodded. "You can't talk to your dad?"

"He's more concerned about my mom than me. It's like I'm invisible."

Finn muttered, "Thank God she doesn't know where Dad was last night."

Violet smiled, weakly. "Thanks for listening. I'm just trying to hold it all together. Someone has to."

"I get it. When my Mimi died, I knew if I unraveled there would be no one to gather up the strands to pull me back together. I didn't realize it at the time, but I held my feelings in so tightly after Mimi died for that reason."

"Exactly," Violet said.

I'd never talked in depth about how it felt to lose Mimi. Like Violet said, there wasn't anyone who really understood. Lisa had barely been surviving, and anyway, she'd never had the capacity to recognize my needs. After Finn died, I had, at least momentarily, let myself go. Thankfully, I'd had Tyler to literally pick me up off the ground.

I wondered if Violet would let me be that person for her. I had to try. "I know you don't know me very well, but I really do understand how you feel. You can talk to me."

"At first, I was so pissed. Now I just feel empty." She looked down at the crumpled napkin in her hand. "But I do keep hearing Finn in my head letting me know that everything is going to be okay."

Finn knelt by his sister. "Everything will be okay," he said. He looked over at me. "Tell her you can see me," he said.

I choked on my drink and involuntarily replied to him with a harsh, "No!" Liquid dribbled down my chin and dripped onto my shirt.

Violet looked startled. "Huh?"

"Oh, just worried about my shirt. I'll be right back."

I rushed in the direction of the bathroom and stuck an ear bud in my ear.

Once we were far enough away from Violet, I asked, "How can she move on when she knows you're still here?" My words came out harder than I'd intended.

Finn reacted as if I'd slapped him. "Is that how you feel?"

"This isn't about me. You know I'm grateful that I can see you, but that's just it—I can see you. They can't. If they knew it just wouldn't seem fair. Besides, do you really think they'd believe me?"

In the bathroom, I turned on the hot water faucet, watching it run while I breathed. I grabbed a paper towel, wet it, and wiped at the small wet spot on my shirt. I wasn't worried about it staining, but I'd needed a reason to get away from Violet. She probably thought I was nuts.

"I don't want us to fight," Finn said.

"Me, either."

The bathroom door opened and Violet walked in, holding both of our drinks. "Hey, Claire. Oh, are you on the phone?"

I nodded, then quickly said, "I'll talk to you later, Julia." I pretended to hang up.

"My dad called. He wants me to come home."

I couldn't imagine he'd be telling her about his night out, but it was good he was home and wanted her there too.

"You should go then," I said.

Violet handed me my half-empty cup; the sides were moist with condensation. She hugged me with her free arm. "I can see why Finn liked you so much. I think you two would've been good together."

"I think so, too." I hugged her back. "You know where to find me if you ever need to talk."

"Okay. Thanks for the voodoo drink order. Oh, and maybe I'll see you at school tomorrow."

"You're going back?" I asked.

"It's time. I keep wanting my mom to move on, so I should try it myself."

"I'll see you at school then." I watched the door close behind her.

"Damn," Finn said.

"I would do anything for you—even this if you really think it's best—but I want you to think hard about it. Telling them that I can see you would bring you back only to take you away again."

"I just want to stop them from falling apart. This is all my fault."

"It's not your fault you died! It's also not your fault how others choose to grieve for you."

Finn frowned.

"Have you ever known someone who died?" I asked.

"My grandparents are all still alive. So, other than me? No."

"It's not something you easily get over. I know you know that, but really, Finn, it hasn't been that long since you died. They can't just go back to normal. Their whole family dynamic has changed. They need time to find their way without you."

He nodded. "I know. I just hate this."

Someone walked into the bathroom. Finn and I quickly stepped out through the open door and began walking to my car.

"I miss Mimi every day. It's gotten easier, but the ache will never fully go away. Think of it this way—it's a testament to the love they had for you that this is so difficult. They will always miss you."

"Will you?" he asked.

"Yes," I said.

"I want you to remember me, but I don't want the memory to hurt. As much as I hate the thought of you with someone else, I want you to have love after me. Even if it's with Tyler."

I stopped. "Finn, you can't stop me from hurting. That can't be your plan for us or the reason you're still here because that's just not possible. And listen up—while I'm sure I'll fall for someone one day, right now you're the only one I want."

"Goodnight, if I had any doubts about why it's you who can see me or why you're on this journey with me, they'd have disappeared after today. You have just put it all into perspective for me."

We gazed at each other, people jostling me and walking through Finn. In each other's eyes, we glimpsed what might've been, but also accepted what we had. I wanted to hold him, to press his body fully against mine. If only the power of my desire for his physical body could make it happen for just a moment.

"I want you so badly," Finn said.

It didn't feel possible to love someone this quickly, but I loved him. Not because he wanted me the way I wanted him, but because he saw all of me and hadn't gone anywhere. Perhaps we'd loved each other in a past life, or maybe time with a ghost was like dog years—each minute like hours, each day like weeks.

Instead of following Violet home, Finn wanted me to take him to where we began.

Our old elementary school was deserted. The classroom lights had long been switched off for the day. The swings swung back and forth, casting long shadows and memories over the sand.

"I don't think I can fit anymore!" I laughed.

"Ah, man! Too bad we can't reenact our first moment together."

I squeezed myself onto the bent rubber and closed my eyes, becoming the girl I'd been on that first day of kindergarten.

Not knowing anyone, I'd spent recess swinging with my hair hiding my face. Lost in my longing for a friend, I was unprepared for the sudden jolt that rocked my then tiny world. I fell in slow motion, colors blurring around me, until I hit the sand with a thump. The brown-haired boy who had unintentionally shoved me stood above me, holding out his hand to help me up. I didn't accept it. A dark-skinned girl ran up to us, pushing him away, asking if I was okay—her offer of friendship immediate.

Finn and Julia had arrived in my life on the same day.

Back in the moment, I tilted my head toward Finn. "You were such a cute kid."

"Oh, no, you were the cute one. Even though girls had cooties back then, I remember thinking how much I liked looking at you. But I never knew how to approach you after that day. You scarred that five-year-old boy when you denied me. I think I always had it in my mind that you'd reject me again."

"I didn't mean to make you feel afraid to talk to me," I said.

"I know that now. I think I just psyched myself out—I thought maybe I wouldn't be enough for you."

"I wasn't sure I'd be enough for you."

"Wow," he said.

"I always thought something would happen between us eventually," I said. "I guess I just imagined that we'd reconnect at our twenty-fifth class reunion or something."

"Who are you kidding? You wouldn't go to a high school reunion!"

We both laughed.

"If I thought there'd be a chance of seeing you there, I wouldn't have missed it."

Finn moved close. "What would you have done if I had just walked up to you in the halls at school, put my hands on your cheeks, pulled your face to mine, and kissed you?"

My stomach flipped at the thought. "I might've fallen over in shock. I'd give almost anything if you could do that right now."

"Ditto," Finn said.

I reached up to Finn's face and held my hand in the air upon his ghostly cheek, his energy meeting mine. "If you'd walked up and kissed me when I was five, ten, or fifteen I would've kissed you back."

"Good to know." His voice was gruff. "I wish I had."

CHAPTER 11

The house was dark when we arrived home. A white paper hung on the TV screen. Lisa had never left me a note before. The tape lifted easily, leaving tiny clumps of glue behind. Words were scribbled sideways on the page, the blue lines ignored.

Claire—
Gone to rehab. Will be gone at least a month.
Left money on the microwave. Call if you need to.

The words were simple and clear, but I had to read the note five times before I was able to wrap my head around what it meant.

"Wow," Finn said.

"Seriously unexpected," I said.

As a kid I'd hovered outside doors, listening to Mimi and Lisa fight. When Mimi begged her to get help, to at least talk to someone, I wondered where Lisa could go and who had the power to make her better by listening to her. The discussions ended, predictably, with Lisa yelling some version of "Get out." Once Mimi nearly tripped over me when she opened the door I'd had my ear pressed against, her eyes wild with a feeling I couldn't name.

"It's a good thing, isn't it?" Finn searched my expression.

What was happening inside me didn't feel like a good thing. My future had been set. Moving away to college had been the light at the long end of my relationship tunnel with Lisa. Now all I saw was a big, blinking question mark. Prior to Mimi dying I would've stayed close to home to remain near her. After her death, Julia became my compass and I redirected myself to where she would be. Then she moved and I had to adjust again. My certain escape from Lisa was all I'd had left to keep me going, and I'd already recalibrated my plan so many times I had no idea how to do it again.

I wondered if this was what Mimi had wanted all along, for Lisa to go away and come back better. If she did change and try to connect with me, wouldn't I have to try, too?

"I don't know." I sat on the couch, still holding the note. "Why now, after all this time?"

Finn sat beside me.

My phone rang. It was Julia FaceTiming. All of the recent events that Julia knew nothing about rushed back to me: Finn's ghost, Finn's dad with Lisa, my conversation with Violet, and now Lisa's unexpected departure. Under regular circumstances, Julia would've known about these things in real time. Since Finn's death, "normal" had jumped the tracks and now I was off-roading.

My first instinct was to hit the decline button, but I clicked the green button instead. When her face appeared on the screen, I ached with missing her and was glad I picked up.

"C! Finally. You're so freaking hard to get a hold of lately," she said.

"Sorry, J. These past few weeks have been..."

"I know, girl. But listen, after the call I had last night, I think it's all about to change for you."

I knew Lisa wasn't in contact with Julia so she couldn't possibly know about that. Besides, Lisa had been with Finn's dad last night.

When I didn't say anything, Julia spoke again. "Hello! Don't you want to know who I talked to?"

There was only one person it could be.

"Tyler," Finn and I said at the same time.

Julia's face lit up. "You got it. Aren't you even a little bit curious to know what he said?"

My capacity for processing new information was at its limit. "Do I have a choice?" I asked.

"Come on, C, ask me what he said."

"Just tell me." My agitation was abundantly clear, but she ignored it.

"Well, he sounded sad."

While I'd never hung up on my best friend before, I wanted to end this call. Worrying about Tyler's heart when mine was shredded was too much. "So, I was busy and didn't hang out with him last night. What's the big deal?"

"It took a while for me to get it out of him, but C, he said he really likes you! He said it's getting harder for him to hide it from you anymore."

"Why is that?" I wished he'd try harder, especially now.

"He's always liked you. And you know how you two connected after Finn died..."

"Do you hear yourself? Finn died. Not that long ago. Died! Did he really expect me to jump into his arms this quickly?"

"You sort of did," she said.

"It wasn't like that." I shook my head, remembering the safety of Tyler's arms, how his voice sounded so close to my ear, and the pressure of his breath on my hair.

Her eyebrows furrowed. "What's wrong? I thought this would make you happy!"

"Seriously? It's too soon."

Julia sighed. "Okay, okay. I thought it would give you hope for the future."

My future was moving beneath me like a treadmill I couldn't slow down. Not knowing when Finn would leave or what would happen with Lisa was part of a future I had no say about. Tyler having feelings for me didn't make me feel hopeful—it felt more like he was slipping away. Now I couldn't lean on him as a friend without confusing him. While my insides clenched at the thought of hurting him, he wasn't my priority.

I sank onto the couch and hugged a cushion to my chest. My throat restricted. I recalled how raw I'd been when Tyler found me in the field. The imperfect pieces of me fully on display—yet oddly, after that, he wanted more of me, not less. Anyone else would probably be flattered by the attention of an attractive, kind and smart guy. Yet listing off adjectives that described him didn't ease the itchiness around my heart or curtail my desire to run from his feelings.

Julia and Finn watched me process.

I shook my head again, trying to push away thoughts of Tyler. "Lisa went to rehab," I said. The tightness in my chest and shoulders loosened a little.

"What? When? Why are you just telling me this now?"

Finn lay beside me, his eyes meeting mine. His nearness paused my unraveling. My love for him warmed me, yet it was now tinged with guilt about Tyler.

I caught Julia up on all that she had missed. Of course, I failed to mention the biggest thing of all, that I was in love with Finn's ghost.

"Wow. That's a lot. And then here I come dumping Tyler all over you."

"You didn't know. Are you supposed to report back to him?"

"I think he expects me to, but you know I'm Team Claire. I'll do whatever you want me to."

"I'll talk to him," I said.

"What will you say?"

"I'm not sure yet."

"Be gentle with him," Julia said. "He's a good guy."

"You know I know that," I said. The holdup was that I already had a good guy. He just happened to be dead and invisible to everyone but me.

Julia and I said our goodbyes.

"I don't want to say I told you so," Finn said after I hung up the phone. "Because a part of me didn't want it to be true."

"If only he'd just been able to keep this to himself. Being friends was enough for me."

"Was it really? Could you say that if I wasn't here with you right now?"

I turned away from him to the ceiling. My eyes traced along the familiar cracks that ran from the edge of the wall to the middle of the room, like lifelines on a hand. "I have no way of knowing," I said.

"He's taking a chance at love."

I nodded. "But…"

"It's no different from us," Finn said. "He's putting out feelers to gauge your feelings. I can't blame the dude for being brave. Besides, he has amazing taste." He smiled.

My lips refused to lift into a smile for him. "What should I do?" I asked.

"What do you want to do?"

"I don't want things to be awkward. I want to stay his friend. I guess what I want is for nothing to change."

"Change is the one thing we can't stop," he said.

"This sucks! Maybe I'll just pretend I don't know," I said.

"Have you ever thought about him as more than a friend?"

There had been occasional moments of attraction, but I hadn't walked the idea through my imagination. I'd never made space for anyone other than Finn. Everything about this conversation seemed unfair. Had Finn still been alive we would've fallen in love and Tyler would've had to curb his feelings forever.

"It's okay if you have, Goodnight."

"It's not that. I mean, I don't know. I'm confused and annoyed with him for doing this now."

"So, his timing isn't the best, but he doesn't know I'm here. He isn't trying to hurt you."

I sighed. Of course, he wasn't trying to hurt me, but why did it feel like he was? "I don't want to talk about him. You're the one I love." It wasn't as if I'd never planned to profess my love for Finn, but I hadn't expected to announce it quite like this.

Finn's face lit up and he flew up to the ceiling, then bounced back down and did his happy dance. I watched him, laughing.

"If you couldn't tell, that was me literally jumping for joy," Finn said, coming back to my side. "I know you're probably thinking it's too soon, but everything about us is on a different plane. Claire Goodnight, I love you too."

My body tingled with giddiness. "I only want you," I said.

"I only want you too, forever," he said.

We cuddled for several minutes in silence.

"Not to take away from our sweet love declarations, but I have to say this. You can be my forever, but I can't be yours. And I'm okay with that. I don't exist in your world anymore—not really. Don't close any doors with Tyler for me."

No matter how true that was, I didn't want to think about it. I just wanted to be a girl in love with a boy, human or not, who loved her back.

"Can't we just pretend, at least for a little while, that we both get forever?" I asked.

"For now," Finn said.

CHAPTER 12

Walking the halls at school the next day, I realized our newly proclaimed love was as invisible as Finn. Not being able to share it with Julia made it feel less real, but she—and the rest of the world—wouldn't believe in our ghostly love story.

I did my best to pay attention in class while Finn wandered the halls. He promised not to disappear without warning, but there was no rulebook and faith in the words of others wasn't a characteristic I could claim. Yet period after period he proved himself by reappearing. Like building blocks, my trust in him began to take form.

The lunch bell rang, and my heart bloomed at the sight of him waiting outside class for me. He rushed through a group of students to get to me.

"Violet's here," he said.

Ever aware of how I appeared to others, I tried to hide the large smile on my face. Being at school for the first time since Finn died couldn't be easy, but it was a good step.

Finn and I walked to my tucked-away lunch spot. Except on rare California rainy days, Julia and I used to eat on the steps behind the theatre. Since she'd moved, I'd begun eating lunch in my car with the windows rolled down. With Finn there, I opted for the shade of the oak trees instead. Students occasionally walked by on the sidewalk in front of us, but we were mostly out of view.

I sat down on the cool concrete steps and put in my earbud.

"Are you working tonight?" Finn asked.

I nodded then pulled my lunch out of my backpack.

"Will Tyler be there?" he asked.

My stomach fluttered at the thought of seeing Tyler. I thought I heard a hint of jealousy in Finn's tone, but it wasn't reflected in his expression.

"He works full time, so yeah, I'm sure he'll be there. Our shifts tend to overlap. I haven't thought about what I'll say to him."

"You can tell him you're in love with a ghost." He beamed at me.

I bit into my sandwich, his attempt at making me laugh missing its mark. "If only it were that easy," I said.

"Oh, look, there's Vi," he said.

Violet lingered several feet away from us in the grass.

"Violet, come on over," I said.

Smiling shyly, she walked up the stairs, wearing a long black sweater over a dark purple skirt with knitted tights. My traditional sweater, jeans and thick black boots were all about comfort and invisibility. I envied her bold personal expression.

"It looked like you might've been on the phone."

"Oh, right." I removed the earpiece. "I seem to be on it a lot lately. How has your day been?"

"No offense, but I'm sort of tired of people asking me how I'm doing," she said. "I think I've answered that question like a hundred times today."

"Right, that must be annoying."

"I think most people are asking out of obligation or aren't sure what else to say—you know? I don't think they want to hear the truth, though. Which is that being here makes me want to cry. Can I like just hide out here with you?"

"Of course. By the way, I like the truth."

"Thank you," she said.

Finn moved out of the way, making space for Violet next to me, but he wasn't quick enough and half of him whooshed through her.

Violet shuddered. "That's weird."

"What is?" I faked confusion.

"You'll think I'm crazy," she said.

"Try me."

"It was like I just felt Finn's spirit. It's almost like he's with you."

I raised my eyebrows at Finn and cleared my throat, unsure how to respond.

"Do I sound nuts?" Violet asked.

"No. I mean, I don't know a lot about spirits, but that doesn't mean they don't exist."

Violet sighed. "I haven't admitted that to anyone—not even my mom, who thinks she can feel him too. Have you felt him?"

I paused, then said, "Maybe."

"Really?" Violet eyes widened behind her glasses.

I nodded. She didn't know me well enough to read my facial expressions and body language, which were immediate giveaways when I told a lie or even a half-truth.

"Do you feel him now?"

"Yes," I said. There was relief in telling just a little bit of truth.

"Finn?" she whispered.

Finn touched her knee with one finger. Violet held her hand out and he quickly backed away.

"What does it feel like to you?" Violet asked.

"I sense his energy."

"To me, it's like I get a sudden rush of him. Like he walked past me or something. Maybe my mom isn't crazy after all, but it's messing with her."

"What does your dad say about it?" I asked.

"Oh! That's why he called me home yesterday. He said that when he got home my mom was sitting on the front porch in her pajamas, whispering Finn's name. When he asked her what she was doing, she told him Finn had been there and touched her."

Finn's shoulders fell forward, and his head dropped to his chest.

"Oh," I said.

"He asked me what we should do. And I thought, *Really, Dad, I'm a fifteen-year-old kid!*" She pulled at her braid then twirled it around her finger. "He mentioned moving."

Finn leaned toward me. "I don't want them to move because of me."

"Do you think you should?" I asked Violet, wanting to reach out to Finn.

"Not really, but maybe it would help? Everywhere I go I look for him. Though I'm not sure it will matter where we are. I'll miss him wherever I am."

"I get that."

"My dad thinks we're losing my mom to grief. I told him that she just needed time. But then he told me about some lady he met who's been grieving for like eighteen years."

"Eighteen years?"

"Yeah, and he said it's really messed up her relationship with her daughter."

The hair on my arms rose. My eyes flashed wildly in Finn's direction, but I was unable to focus on his face. The lady had to be Lisa. A tornado of questions spun through my head. It was as if a key that I hadn't been looking for dropped into my hand. Somewhere there was a door waiting to be unlocked.

Finn moved close to me. "Goodnight?" he asked.

His voice brought me back to the present. Lisa was gone. I couldn't rush home to ask about this supposed grief.

"Is everything okay?" Violet asked.

I turned back to her. "Uh, yes. Do what you can to help your mom. I'm sure that's what Finn would want you to do."

"Thanks, Claire." Violet smiled.

I stood, feeling a sudden desire to run. "I have to go."

Violet looked confused. "Oh, okay."

"We'll talk later," I said.

I slung my backpack over my shoulder and hurried toward the parking lot, my heart thudding.

Finn was at my heels, and then he was in front of me, floating backward. "Goodnight, where are you going?"

"Where does your dad work?" I asked.

"Wait, what? Why?"

"You heard Violet! I'm going to find out what he knows about Lisa."

"I don't think things are supposed to unfold this way," Finn said.

I stopped. "What do you mean?" My voice shook.

The end-of-lunch bell blared, and a flow of students began to move toward their classrooms, Finn dodging back and forth to avoid them. Not caring if I was in anyone's way, I stood in place. A shriek that was forming deep inside me threatened to escape.

I began running again. Out of breath by the time I got to the edge of the parking lot, I hunched over, gasping. Finn put his hand on my back, unaffected by the run. Betrayal loomed between us.

I brushed him away. "Why don't you seem surprised by this?"

Finn's expression froze.

"Finn!"

"I only overheard part of their conversation. It didn't make sense to me, so I didn't tell you."

Anger burned hot beneath my skin. "What did you hear?"

"Lisa said she was a horrible mother."

Lisa acknowledging her parenting faults wasn't something I'd seen coming. But Finn keeping things from me wasn't either. "What was the grief about?"

"I don't know," he said. "I walked in near the end of their conversation."

I rolled my eyes at him. He wasn't perfect after all. "You had to have heard more—gotten a sense of something."

"There was a pain in her admitting her faults. She was crying and seemed heartbroken, but I didn't hear why."

I stared at him open-mouthed, remembering waking up alone under my willow tree the other night and then finding Finn inside.

"Why didn't you tell me about any of it? Why did you lie about why you were in the house?"

"I was caught off guard—and I knew you'd go to Lisa to fill in the gaps. Then you'd have to explain how you'd overheard them talking. I was trying to protect you—and us."

"You told me you loved me, but you couldn't tell me this?" Clearly, our paranormal love wasn't immune from the typical relationship messiness.

"It's not like that. I had no idea she'd take off for rehab the next day. I thought she'd talk to you about it."

"Why do you think she'd suddenly talk to me now, after all this time?"

"I guess I didn't think it through."

"I need space. Back off as much as you can."

"What are you going to do?"

"I guess I won't be going to see your dad." I spewed sarcastic word-bullets at him, attempting to hurt him like he'd hurt me. "But I don't want you with me."

My words hit their mark and his eyes reflected the pain in both of us. I didn't care.

CHAPTER 13

My harsh words to Finn vibrated in my chest. For the first time since he'd appeared as a ghost, I didn't crave his sparky nearness and my stomach didn't clench up at the thought of never seeing him again. But I didn't want to be alone with the noise inside my head either.

In my car, I flipped through several radio stations until I found one that matched my mood. Heavy metal. I turned up the volume. As I drove, the steering wheel became my drum. I shook my head to the beat of the screeching guitars and hard beats. My blood pumped fast, and my heart kept time to the beat.

I honked at a car driving too slowly in front of me. Before the driver had a chance to move out of my way, I changed lanes without using my blinker. Speeding up to pass it, I glared at the grandpa-aged driver then turned up the volume.

Finn had to be close by, his shimmering form pulled along behind me, but I didn't look in the rear-view mirror. For the first time since he'd come back to me as a ghost, I didn't want to see him.

It had taken Finn dying to finally give me a name to the ugly thing that had filled the house my whole life. Grief had been the unspoken presence—larger than me, Lisa and Mimi combined.

I wanted to uncover Lisa's buried grief—lift the rug it had been swept beneath and see the dust of it floating in the sunlit air, free.

And then there was Mimi's betrayal—keeping her illness from me, robbing us of a real goodbye. Perhaps I shouldn't have been surprised that Mimi chose to keep whatever Lisa was grieving from me. Unable to fix anything with her daughter, maybe the ancient secret had weighed heavily on her and had literally become the cancer that ate her to death.

If she was alive, I could yell at her. Stand in front of her demanding an explanation. Even if the truth wasn't hers to share, hadn't she loved me enough to give it to me?

My skin no longer seemed secure enough to hold my body together. One wrong move and I would melt away. I needed someone else's strength to hold me in one piece until I could do it myself. Without realizing it, I'd driven to the only person who could help. My heart lifted a little at the sight of Tyler's car in the parking lot of Palm Row Pizza.

Adapting to the silence that echoed through me louder than the music had, I let my tears fall until I felt somewhat normal again.

At the door, I realized that running into Tyler's arms wasn't fair. But it was too late. Tyler was at the front of the store. Expecting a customer, he looked up, a forced customer-greeting-smile on his face that dropped to a frown when he saw me.

He hopped over the counter, put his hands on my shoulders, and searched my eyes for answers. The familiar smells and sounds of the place, and him, cocooned me in a version of coming home.

"What's wrong?"

Unwilling to tell him that I was there because my ghost boyfriend betrayed me, I blubbered something unintelligible.

Tyler typed in the code to get us into the back of the restaurant, and with his arm around me led us to the manager's office.

He called out to the only other employee in the building. Weekdays were always slow. "Hey, I'm going to take a break! Can you man everything for a while?"

A male voice yelled back, "Sure."

The small room contained a desk and swivel chair. Several clipboards hung by nails on the wall, gripping crinkled schedules and inventory sheets. Tyler closed the door and led me to an old loveseat crammed into the corner. I sat, slipping down lower than I'd been prepared for into the saggy brown cushions.

Tyler paused briefly, looking from the chair to the couch, before opting to sit down next to me. His weight on the cushions pulled me close to him and he wrapped his muscular arm around my shoulders, enclosing me. My ear folded, pressing into his chest. The boom of his heart pounded against my cheek.

A flicker of guilt drifted within me, but my need for human touch outweighed everything else. He pulled back, trying to look at my face, but I turned away, leaning into him harder. He squeezed me again, and—falling into a safe place—I cried. Eventually, I'd need to come up with an explanation for why I wasn't at school, for why I couldn't stop crying, but for now, he didn't ask.

Several minutes passed. With closed eyes, I listened to Tyler's sturdy breathing. My body began to feel solid again and my chest rose and fell in time to his.

"Claire." He spoke into my hair.

There was longing in his tone, in the way his heart was beating, and in the way he held me. I didn't have the emotional capacity to respond to it, so I ignored it.

I attempted to sit up straight on the couch and remove myself from his hug, but the cushion shifted me back to him again. The need for an explanation had come and I scrambled to bypass the truth, telling him about Lisa going to rehab.

When I said her name, my body stiffened and I wanted to punch the old couch, the shiny white walls—and even Tyler, for having feelings for me that I didn't know how to deal with. Instead, I just sat there clenching my fists on my lap.

"I'm glad you came to me," he said quietly.

"You're the only friend I've got right now," I emphasized the word friend.

He released me, took off his hat, and ruffled his hair around. The messiness of it reminded me of Finn's forever bedhead.

Tyler opened his mouth to speak just as Finn walked through the closed door. Finn moved forward quickly then disappeared. Tyler cupped both hands on either side of my face. The electricity of his touch tingled on my skin. Confused, I gripped his wrists, trying to free myself.

Tyler shifted toward me and whispered, "Goodnight, it's me."

Each hair on my body rose in reaction to the impossible. Tyler had never called me that. I searched Tyler's eyes and saw a slight hint of Finn's behind Tyler's blue ones. "How?" The pressure of his hands on my face sent shivers up my spine.

"I'm not sure," Finn said, using Tyler's voice.

"No!" I pushed my flat palms against his chest. Finn being able to enter and control someone's body wasn't something I'd ever considered, and not one part of it felt right. "Get out of him!" My voice sounded like a growl.

"I need to talk to you," Finn said.

"Talk to me as you. Not as Tyler!"

"Goodnight, please—you have to believe that I didn't mean to hurt you," he said.

"This is exactly why I don't let people in," I snapped. "I always get hurt."

Tyler's body shook beside me, his eyes focused straight ahead, his face and hands clenched. Finn seemed to gain control of Tyler's body again, and it relaxed.

"This isn't the way to win my forgiveness." I glared at him.

"I only want to do right by you." He gently placed his hand on mine.

I held my breath to stop myself from screaming.

Confronting someone with my feelings wasn't something I'd ever done. For years I just lived the status quo—silent, accepting. But this time I refused to just disappear beneath my turtle shell. "You have to let me be mad," I said.

My body begged for something to plug the gaping hole in my chest. I imagined bottling the feelings back up, pressing a cork into the wound, like I'd wanted to do with all the wine bottles Lisa opened. But that would only be a temporary fix.

I looked into Tyler's eyes, finding Finn there again. Heat rushed through my body and all the desire that had been building for Finn's touch burst out of my pores. I knew he hadn't meant to hurt me, but he had. His words and his almost-there eyes worked to poke holes in the mad parts of me.

"Cross my heart and hope to die I will never hurt you again," he said. "I guess that phrase doesn't work too well in my condition, but you get the point."

If I forgave him, just for a second, then I could have a piece of him again. I touched my fingers to Tyler's lips, remembering Finn's.

"This might be our only chance. I really want to kiss you," he said.

My thoughts raced and my body begged for some sort of relief. Yet kissing Finn meant kissing Tyler. It meant Tyler's lips, stand-ins for Finn's, on mine.

"No!"

He'd kept things from me. And now he was possessing Tyler. Another betrayal.

Finn wiped the tears from my face, and I wanted to feel more of him on my skin. What if we never got another chance to touch each other like this?

I leaned forward slightly and Finn, in Tyler's body, closed the distance between us, his lips hot on mine.

Tyler's energy pressed in, reminding me that it wasn't just Finn kissing me, not really. The mixture of all three of us drifted awkwardly between us. I squeezed my eyes shut, trying to push Tyler from my mind—replace him with Finn again. Instead of sinking deeper into what was left of Finn, I couldn't erase the disgust stewing in my stomach.

"No!" I pulled away, then pushed Tyler's chest, hard.

Finn writhed inside of Tyler. "I can't hold him much longer."

"I don't want you to! Let him go!"

"Goodnight, please…"

"No, Finn! Get out, get out, get out!"

I gripped Tyler's shirt. Tyler was strong, but I was mad. I shook him hard, working to force Finn out.

Wide-eyed, Finn exited Tyler's body. "You pushed me out!"

"Good." I glared up at him.

Tyler mumbled, his eyes dazed. I released my hands from his shirt and stood. He looked confused, and raised his hand to his mouth, touching his lips. The lips that had just been on mine.

"What…what just happened?" Tyler asked.

I shifted on my feet, not meeting his gaze.

He hit both hands against his chest, Tarzan-like, as if reconnecting to the solidity of his body. "Were you pushing me?" His voice was high.

"Um…" I said.

"I was hugging you, and then…it's like I blacked out."

I muttered to Finn under my breath, "If you hadn't kept things from me, we wouldn't be here."

"What's going on?" Tyler asked. "Did I try to kiss you?"

I looked down at my feet.

"Oh, my God," he said.

Not willing to let him believe that, I shook my head.

"I didn't?" Relief edged into his voice.

"I kissed you but…I didn't mean to."

"You didn't mean to?"

"That didn't come out right. I was upset, and I guess I got caught up in the moment…"

"But then you pushed me away?" He stood up, wobbling briefly before centering himself.

I stepped back and Finn moved out of the way. The three of us stood in the small room, forming a triangle.

There was a knock on the door. We all jumped.

"Boss, the phone is ringing, but I have to take this delivery." A male voice spoke through the door.

"Yup, I'll be right there," Tyler said. He put his hand to his head. "Why can't I remember any of this?"

Regret splintered through me like the cracked tiles beneath Finn's feet. Finn reached for me, but I shifted away and moved to touch Tyler's shoulder. After meeting his dark gaze, I stopped before making contact. "Are you okay?" I asked.

The phone rang on the speakers throughout the store, loud and intrusive.

"I don't know, but then I'm not sure how much you really care anyway, Claire."

He'd flung his words like I'd done earlier with Finn. We both deserved it.

He paused before leaving the room, seemingly waiting for an explanation, an apology—something. Silence surrounded us, holding us hostage momentarily. I was being given time to come clean. It hurt like hell to let him think I kissed him then pushed him away.

"It was Finn," I said, quietly.

I hadn't planned to say it, but how could I say nothing after what had just happened?

"Really? You're going with that?"

"If you'd let me explain."

"I don't want to listen to some insane explanation as to why you didn't want to kiss me."

He sighed, opening the door with a force that sent it into the wall. A doorknob-shaped mark remained. Tyler disappeared around the corner.

Ignoring Finn's eyes, I rushed toward the exit with my head down.

Later that night, I sat on the couch processing the day. When I'd returned to work after the Finn and Tyler incident, Tyler had been gone. The part-time assistant manager was there in his place. I knew I was the reason he'd left early and that made me want to throw up.

Finn hovered nearby as I wrapped my arms around my bent legs and rocked. A fast run to release the stress of the day would've helped, but it was dark and too late. My eyes begged to close, so I closed them.

Finn wanted to talk about the kiss and the possession he'd taken of Tyler's body. But I didn't.

"I feel horrible," Finn said.

I'd barely spoken to Finn since we'd left Tyler that afternoon. I wanted to disappear into myself beneath my willow tree and filter through everything, but the effort to move was too much.

A part of me understood. If I'd walked in on him and Kelly holding each other I likely would've jumped too, without thinking about her or the consequences. But it wasn't me who'd done it—it was Finn.

"You should feel horrible, Finn. You can't just do something like that without consent."

"You're right. If someone did that to you or Violet, I'd be pissed. You told me to get out and I didn't listen."

"I told him it was you," I said.

I hadn't realized the weight I'd been carrying until it wasn't all mine anymore—even if Tyler didn't understand what I meant—that Finn was here as a ghost and what he had done.

"You sort of told him."

"Maybe I should've tried harder to explain."

"He was too hurt to hear you."

I looked at Finn, really looked at him for the first time since the incident. He shone less vibrantly, looked more see-through.

"You're less here," I said.

"Using Tyler's body took a lot of energy," Finn said. "Maybe that's our punishment—my punishment, lost time with each other."

My heart clenched. Another rule to add to our rule book. "We'd deserve that."

"You don't deserve it." Finn's face fell even more. "Besides, I have more to do."

"Like what?"

"Fix us, for one. And then I need to make sure everyone else is on the path to being okay."

"Everyone?"

"You, Lisa, my family...Tyler," he said. "I don't know exactly what I mean by okay, but I think I'll know when it happens."

I wasn't sure Finn, or I had the tools required to break through the instant wall that had risen between me and Tyler. And Lisa? Everything in me shut down at the thought of her, not wanting to face what it was that made me unworthy of her love.

"What if we're all lost causes?" I asked.

"None of you are lost causes."

I leaned back and closed my eyes. I was tired but not sleepy—overwhelmed, and numb.

Eventually, I staggered to my feet and told Finn I wanted to sleep alone.

"If it means anything, I know for sure that Lisa and my dad didn't sleep together," he said.

Instead of feeling relieved, I realized this was another thing that had been purposely kept from me. Another reason to stay mad.

"Why did you wait to tell me?"

"Everything I say will sound like an excuse. If I wasn't a ghost, you wouldn't have known about any of it, and I felt some strange obligation to the universe, or whatever, to let it come out on its own."

I wasn't sure if I could argue with the universe, but him saying nothing still stung.

"What else did you see or hear?" I asked.

"Not much. They were in Lisa's room, but they were fully clothed. I hadn't been there long before I heard you come back into the house. I rushed out and besides, I already felt guilty listening to their conversation in the first place. Being a ghost isn't all it's cracked up to be," he sighed. "I still hate that he was with her in her bedroom and that he was even here at all."

"Me too."

"I'd like to know what even led him to her."

"I plan to find out when Lisa gets back. It doesn't look great, but at least they didn't sleep together. That must be a relief."

He nodded. "I'm so sorry, Goodnight, for everything."

Torn between wanting to understand where he was coming from and still feeling mad that he'd kept things from me, and had taken over Tyler's body, I asked him to give me space.

He told me he loved me and left my room.

Once I was alone, I sent two text messages.

One to Lisa: *I have some questions for you.*

The other to Tyler: *Are you okay? Are we okay?*

I looked heavenward and said, "Can you hear me, Mimi? Eighteen years of grief for Lisa? What don't I know?"

My mind whirled with questions and when no answers came by text or otherwise, I finally fell asleep.

CHAPTER 14

In the near dark of Lisa's closet, I held still, listening for Mimi. Her voice moved from room to room, calling out, "Claire, where are yoooouuu?"

Lisa's room was off limits, but I'd grown tired of my usual hiding spots. When I heard Mimi shuffling down the hallway in my direction I shifted deeper into the tiny space, pressing up against a cardboard box. We had many boxes like this one, but they were all in the garage and were filled with books.

Quietly, I unfolded the flaps, the smell of dust sneaking out. I stuck my hand inside and touched something small and soft, and pulled out a tiny teddy bear. It was just like the one I had tucked under the blankets on my bed, except that this bear was still soft and fuzzy, unlike the loved-down fuzz on my own bear.

"Claire, where are you?"

I jumped at the sound of her voice so close, my elbow banging against the wall. "Oof." I rubbed at the sore spot.

Suddenly the door slid open, exposing me to the bright light and Mimi's angry eyes.

"You're not to be in here." She bent down and grabbed my arm, then dragged me to my feet. The bear fell from my lap and stared blankly up at the ceiling.

Mimi picked it up. It dangled helplessly before she forced it back into the stuffy box. Grunting, she picked up the box and hefted it above her and placed it on the shelf above Lisa's clothes.

I gazed up, knowing I'd never be able to reach it. "Is that my bear?" I asked.

Breathing hard, Mimi slid the door shut with a bang of finality and dropped to her knees. We were eye to eye.

"What's the matter?" I asked.

"Nothing," she said. "Everything is okay. Everything is okay."

When someone said something twice like that, I knew the opposite was true.

"But, Mimi, why isn't that bear in my room?"

"It's not yours." She shifted her eyes away and stood up. "Let's go make some cookies." She touched my shoulder, shooing me and my questions out.

"Wait!" I yelled into the darkness of my room after waking.

Mimi was gone. It had been a dream. I was no longer five years old, but me again, just weeks shy of my eighteenth birthday.

Finn rushed in from wherever he'd been, which couldn't have been far. "Did you have a nightmare?"

I rubbed my eyes and shook away the years that had passed in an instant. "It was a memory in a dream."

"What was the memory?" His proximity and gaze were timid.

"A box, a bear and Mimi."

I remembered that day. Shortly after that, I'd stopped asking Mimi questions and had started spending more time under my tree. Now, though, I was literally tall enough to unravel the mystery for myself.

I threw back the covers and headed for Lisa's old closet. After Mimi died, Lisa moved into Mimi's room, but maybe the box was still there. When I pulled open the door, Mimi's clothes were hanging inside, and her shoes were lined up neatly on the floor, as if she were still around to step into them. I ran my fingers along the fabric of her favorite knitted sweater. A surge of missing her slammed into me.

I'd been unaware that Lisa had taken the time to carefully move everything and stage it like this, into a shrine of sorts. Maybe this had been her way of holding onto her mom the only way she knew how—with things.

"Do you see it?" Finn asked.

Still stuck between sleep and dreaming, I shook my head.

I turned the knob of the master bedroom and remembered the times I'd run in there after a bad dream to jump into Mimi's bed. After I'd settled down, she'd never sent me back to my own room. Instead, she'd wrapped me up in blankets and pulled me close to her. Sleepily asking about my dreams. She'd always said that dreams were our brains bringing our subconscious thoughts to the surface. If only she were here to lie beside me now. Or maybe she was and had brought the memory to me.

Both sides of the blankets were down on Lisa's bed, a reminder that she hadn't been alone the night before she left for rehab. Though, per Finn, they'd only shared the bed and not each other. Her dresser drawers were halfway open and dirty laundry was piled up in the corner.

High-heeled shoes in red, pink, black and blue were tangled among each other on the floor. Blouses, sweaters, skirts, and dresses dangled in her closet. After shifting some of her clothing out of the way, I spotted the box tucked away in the back corner. The bear was the first thing I saw when I pulled open the lid. All these years later it was still there, alone, and unloved.

I carefully carried the box to my room, placed it on my bed then backed away. Somehow, I knew its contents were about to blow up my whole life.

Finn watched me from a short distance away.

My own bear had been tucked away and I took it out. The fur was rough from years of cereal spills and tears. Once I'd become a teenager, I kept him in my nightstand and only cuddled with him when I was sad. For months after Mimi died, he'd found a home again, smushed against my neck at night.

I placed the two bears together, a matching pair, reunited.

The next thing I pulled from the box was a frame containing a picture of a youthful Lisa with shiny eyes and brown hair. She was with a young man about her age. His hair was dark and combed to the side. He sat on a chair, and she stood behind him, one hand on his shoulder—a department store studio pose. There was something familiar about him, but I wasn't sure what.

Finn sucked in his breath. "He looks like you."

It made sense that he saw the resemblance. He spent more time seeing me than I saw myself. On second glance, I noticed that we both had oval faces and high cheekbones. My hands quivered. "Maybe?" I asked.

"He must be..."

"My dad." These were words I never thought I'd say. His face was something I never thought I'd see.

I pulled out several manila envelopes filled with pictures. The photos fluttered out like dying leaves falling from a tree. I wanted to flick the smile off Lisa's face. Wanting information on my dad, I flipped through the photos so quickly that some of them fell to the floor, slipping beneath my bed.

Then, there it was, scrawled on the back of a photo in Mimi's flowery, cursive handwriting. I closed my eyes, thanking her for giving me another answer.

Benjamin.

No last name.

Mimi's last name was Goodnight, so I hadn't even been given his name. The possibilities for where my dad could be were endless. As a child, the many questions I'd asked Mimi were met with "Shush" or "We'll talk about it later." But we never did. The unknowns locked away inside me for years now demanded a response.

Next, I pulled out two small boxes with clear plastic lids, two white onesies, each with a name embroidered on the front in pink cursive: *Claire* and *Sophia*.

Sophia?

Maybe they'd picked two names and had outfits made with both choices. If that was the case, it was strange that mine was still pristine. My heart sank at the thought that perhaps Sophia was the intended owner of the other bear. She'd obviously never received it. I removed the lid containing the onesie and traced my fingers across the letters. Sophia.

The possibilities rushed around in my brain, making my head hurt. Two names. Two bears. Were there supposed to be two of us?

While I'd always felt like someone important had been missing from my life, I'd assumed the absence had belonged to a father, not a sibling. Not a...twin? The ache of losing something I'd never had reminded me of losing Finn, but this was deeper, emptier. The losses of my life landed around me like rocks settling after a landslide, heavy and on new ground.

Before I'd fallen asleep, I'd asked for Mimi's help with what Lisa's grief was about. It was as if Mimi had sent me the dream that led me to this box containing pieces of a past, I knew nothing about.

It was late but I knew I'd never fall back to sleep, not without some answers. The remaining envelopes were full of pictures of Lisa and Benjamin, a chronicle of their relationship. There had to be more information somewhere. I closed my eyes and rubbed my fingers on my temples. Finn's energy field inched closer.

"No," I said.

"I'm here for you, Claire."

"This is all too much."

"Do you want me to go?"

"Yes. No. Of course, I don't want you to go, but I'm still mad and I need to think."

Finn disappeared out of the window.

Lisa would know the answers. I'd already texted her without reply. Sure, it was late, but I wondered if she'd even get back to me at all.

Documents. Maybe there were documents in the house to explain the two names, the two bears, and the smiling young man who looked like me. I wondered if Sophia and Benjamin were out there somewhere—and if so, why weren't we all together? Or had something happened to one or both of them?

A memory of Mimi opening mail and paying bills flashed through my mind. My socked feet raced down the stairs and didn't stop until I was standing in front of her large roll-top desk. Lisa never sat here. Mimi had overseen all the important things in our lives. The answers had to be here.

A drawer at a time, I pulled out papers and quickly scanned them. After several minutes, I paused looking at the pile of useless information spread around me. There was one more drawer left. If this was another dead end, I would have to rely on Lisa for information. I opened it to find clearly labeled and alphabetized file folders. It didn't take long for me to come across the one marked Baby.

Two unsealed white envelopes were all that was inside. The first one contained a thick beige official-looking paper. Once unfolded, I discovered it was my birth certificate. No surprises there. Everything looked accurate. My last name was listed as Goodnight. The father field was blank.

My stomach dropped at the header of the next document. Instead of claiming itself as a Birth Certificate, it listed Death Certificate in dark cursive letters. The name on the form was Sophia Goodnight. No father listed there either.

The something missing from my life had been her.

I looked at the dates. "She died the same day we were born."

Sophia was gone, but I didn't know how or why. I wondered if my dad was gone too. Really gone, like she was. Lisa was such a mess she'd probably done something to cause this.

Back upstairs, I grabbed my phone from my bedside table and scrolled to Lisa's name. I didn't care how late it was—I needed to know what happened. After only one ring the call went to voicemail. I hung up.

The mere task of breathing was hard. Finn was suddenly beside me again.

"What can I do?" Finn asked.

I had no idea what I needed.

Finn put his hands on my cheeks but I pulled away. The merging of him and Tyler was still too fresh and unresolved.

I considered the fact that I had a twin. "Aren't twins supposed to know things about each other?"

"There is no way you could've remembered this," he said. "Maybe you hold your hand in your sleep because you used to hold hers..."

I had no way of knowing if my loneliness was different from anyone else's but losing the person I had grown beside for nine months would've left a mark that I had no words for. My body and soul had been carrying the knowledge that my memory couldn't hold.

And what about my dad? "Either Lisa pushed Benjamin away or he's dead too. Otherwise, why wouldn't he be here with me?"

Finally, I let myself fully look at Finn. The sadness bubbling up inside of me was also on his face and in the depths of his eyes.

Unable to relax, I showered. The water scorched my skin to a blotchy red while I leaned against the cool white tile. I couldn't even cry. The truth was more surreal than anything I could've imagined, and I couldn't wrap my head around it.

Clutching both bears, I fell asleep around five am. Finn asked if he could stay with me so I wouldn't be alone. I allowed it but turned my back to him.

The next morning, my phone woke me up before my alarm went off. Groaning, I focused on the number calling, but didn't recognize it or even the area code. Remembering that I'd called Lisa late last night, I picked up. "Hello?"

"Am I speaking with Claire Goodnight?" a stern female voice asked.

"Yes, that's me," I said.

"My name is Jane. Your mother is staying at our facility. She noticed a missed call from you and asked me to make sure you were okay."

"Right." I wondered why Lisa hadn't called me herself, but I wasn't surprised.

"Well, are you okay, dear?"

"I am. Um, I just had something to ask her."

"Is it a terribly important question, dear? Are you in need of anything dire?"

I paused, contemplating the word "dire" in relation to what I had learned. I'd survived not knowing all my life, so no, it wasn't exactly dire. I could think of other words I would use to describe what I was going through, but dire? No.

The official voice said, "It's just that she's only been here a short time, and unless an interruption is absolutely necessary, we'd prefer to keep her on her current healing trajectory."

I heard a clicking noise and imagined Jane on the other end of the line impatiently tapping a pen against her desk.

I'd never needed anything from Lisa before and didn't see a reason to change that now. I would leave her to her "current healing trajectory" and, like always, handle mine on my own.

"Please allow her to continue on her path as is." I feigned a tone of importance, like Jane's. Even now, in her failure to call me herself, the sting of Lisa's rejection hit me pointedly in the center of my heart.

"As long as you're okay, dear. We want to ensure that you're safe and well taken care of."

"Let her know that this dear is continuing to take care of herself. Nothing new there. Goodbye." I hung up before Jane could respond. I wouldn't be making another attempt to contact Lisa. Even if it was dire.

CHAPTER 15

It took over a week for me to tell Julia about my discovery. On the same call, I also had to explain that Tyler probably wasn't returning her texts because of me. He still hadn't returned mine and had rearranged his schedule to ensure I never saw him at work. I hated not seeing him and not being able to explain.

Julia called me back an hour after we hung up. "Dad said he'd pay for you to fly out here. And you can stay as long as you want."

"You told them?" My voice rose.

"Of course I did," she said. "You're part of the family."

"No, I'm a charity case."

Even if I'd wanted to go, I wouldn't have. I wasn't convinced Lisa would stick out rehab. I'd waited long enough for the truth and couldn't miss her return. Until then I was better off alone.

"What the hell, Claire?" Julia asked.

"You've all felt sorry for me for years," I said.

The Morgans had always been marvelous to me. They'd invited me to dinners and so many sleepovers. During pool parties, Mr. Morgan had thrown me up in the air the same way he did with Julia and her brothers, but none of that made me one of them. There had always been a gap between them and me, and it had grown wider since they'd left me behind.

"You know that's not true."

"I'm fine on my own." My legs itched with a desire to run. It was the only way to calm the wild, anxious creature inside me.

"Stop being stupid. You're not alone."

"I have to go." I hung up the phone and jammed it in my pocket before running barefoot down the stairs and out the front door.

My phone rang again immediately. Without looking I picked it up. "I don't want to talk anymore."

"Excuse me? Is this Claire Goodnight?" Jane from rehab. I'd never forget the way she spoke.

"Oh, it's you. What do you want?"

Finn watched me from the doorway. I hated the way he was seeing me and the way I was acting. He probably didn't recognize me anymore. My body ached to run.

"I'm calling to give you the details for family day next Saturday."

I'd seen enough movies to know what that entailed. Even though I wanted answers, I refused to show up for her and listen to her apologies when she'd ignored me my whole life.

"You must have the wrong number. Please don't call again."

I cried as I ran, and didn't stop until my feet ached, my sides screamed, and my breath came out in gasps. Finn pulled along behind me due to our connection but remained at a distance.

He'd had no choice but to endure my mood swings and silent treatment. The walls that had tumbled down when Finn appeared as a ghost were now higher than ever. Pushing people away was what I did when things got hard.

Panting as I walked back home, I wondered what the freaking point of my life was. Finn stepped in line beside me. He couldn't leave, but he was still there, unwavering. Still loving. I didn't deserve it. His expression softened and his gaze reminded me that I mattered. Even when I didn't want to see it, love, his eyes said, —love is the point of your life.

I wasn't sure I could believe him.

My feet were sore the next morning, but I still planned to run.

"You've been running so much, Goodnight. Have you ever been on a hike?"

I stopped tying my shoes. "No."

"Let's go to the mountains."

Pleased to be given a new way to distract myself, I agreed.

I dumped loose pens and books out of my backpack, then filled it up with water bottles and snacks. I dug around in Lisa's closet and found a pair of what looked to be hiking boots. Finn said they had a nice tread. I pressed my foot inside, surprised to learn that we wore the same size.

Curving back and forth up the mountain, we drove for just under an hour. The pure blue sky was etched with flecks of white clouds. Surrounded by nature, I felt the anxiety of waiting for Lisa's return home ease.

A large wooden sign with yellow letters labeled the trail. We followed the path made flat and obvious by those who had gone before. As I pushed my body up the hills and over swift streams my mind began to empty.

Finn broke our silence by pointing out several burnt trees that had been moved off to the side. "A few years ago, this whole area was ravaged by a fire. Almost everything burned. My family and I used to hike up here all the time. It was sad to watch it burning on the news."

Despite their charcoal trunks, the trees continued to grow, and flowers boldly bloomed against their black, peeling bark. I envied how nature recovered after devastation. It didn't hold grudges or live in the past. It didn't have to forgive, it just kept on growing.

Several miles into the hike, I stopped in awe. A field of oversized dandelions, some the size of tennis balls, sprouted in the tall, wild grass.

"How did you know?" I asked.

Finn raised his eyebrows.

"About the dandelions," I said.

It was a dandelion-lovers dream come true. Strands of grass tickled my fingers as I weaved through the field until I found a perfectly circular dandelion whose stem was just a foot shorter than me. The large puff contained at least ten wishes compared to an average-sized one.

This field of wishes had to be a sign; a reminder of how long I'd wanted Finn and how still being mad at him was wasting the chance I'd been given.

I sank to my knees. Damp earth pressed into my pants.

"Goodnight?" Finn slunk down beside me.

Something shifted. My heart cracked open in the mountain air. I don't know if it was the trees or the dandelions that brought me back, but for the first time since that day with Tyler I looked at my ghost boyfriend and allowed myself to love him.

"I wished for you," I said.

"You did?" He tilted his head to the side.

"You were the only thing I ever wished for." I looked up at the dandelion that towered above me.

He put his hand on his heart. "Are you still glad you got your wish?"

"Hell, yes," I said.

His eyes glowed bright with the sunlight filtering through them. "Even after everything that happened?"

"Absolutely. Everything sucks right now, but I wouldn't change my wish," I said. "Any regrets about being stuck here with me?"

"Being with you is the only place I want to be even when you're mad at me."

"Do you think this was what Mimi had in mind by keeping you here?" I asked.

"I have a feeling it's exactly what she had in mind. Hey, why don't you make a wish now? You can wish for something or someone else now."

Asking for the impossible like Finn coming back to life would be wasteful. Bringing back my sister or Mimi was also in the realm of things that couldn't be done. Wishing for my dad didn't feel plausible either.

Everything I'd thought I wanted had changed. All I knew was that there was no going back. Wanting to would only stop me from moving forward.

I lay down and placed my hands beneath my head. Like my future, the endless blue sky stretched out above me, blank and full of possibilities.

Finn leaned back too and propped his head up with his elbow. "You're the most beautiful thing I've ever seen," he said.

"No, you are." I rolled on my side, mirroring his position.

"Do you want to talk?" He touched the tip of my nose with his finger.

"How much time have you got?" I asked.

"For you? Forever," he said.

"I'm sorry I've been shutting you out," I said.

"It's okay, Goodnight," he said.

His fading color glowed brighter than it had been. Maybe it was due to our sunlit hike or maybe it was me. Whatever it was, I felt my soul unfold like a red carpet and I wanted him to know everything.

"Has your heart ever felt so broken it was like it had literally shattered?" I asked.

Finn shook his head.

"Mine did the day you died. But it was about more than that. It was about Lisa, Julia, and Mimi. It was about everything I felt but didn't know." I described how I'd literally howled for him until I lost my voice, and how Tyler came when I called.

Finn listened without speaking, his eyes soft, his mouth turned down.

I flicked away my tears. "In case I don't get another chance to say it, I wanted you to know that you being here saved me."

"I think we saved each other." He lifted his eyes to mine and put his hand on my cheek.

I pushed away the memory of Tyler and pressed into his energy.

"I knew Tyler was a good guy." He looked away from me and up at the dandelion.

"Yes," I said.

"He sees you," Finn said.

"You see me!"

"I just got lucky—well if dying is lucky. Who I am now isn't the person I would've been when I was alive."

"What do you mean?"

"When I was alive, I wouldn't have had an all-access, behind-the-scenes view of you. I would've gotten to know you in small doses and maybe you wouldn't have let me in. This way it was easier for you to show me all of you."

"If you'd lived you would've seen me eventually. I would've opened up," I said.

"We don't know that for sure. This way I got to see that you've become a turtle, as Julia says, to protect yourself. I'm not sure I would've understood that before." He paused. "I'm just trying to say that I'm not the perfect person you thought I was. Tyler gets you, even without the full picture."

"I don't know—even with your faults, you're still amazing to me. Besides, Tyler doesn't want anything to do with me anymore," I said.

"That's just temporary."

I stood, wiped the grass from my legs, and with it the subject of Tyler. "Thank you for bringing me here."

"You drove!" He smiled. "So, do you still believe in wishes?"

To me, wishes and hope were the same thing. No matter how hopeless my upbringing made me feel, I didn't want to give up on hoping for something better. Somewhere between dandelions, my repeated wish for Finn had come true. Choosing not to believe in the power of the universe that provided me with this magical second chance with Finn would be crazy.

"I do," I said.

The dandelion before me was the perfect height. There was no need to pluck the tall, thick stem from the earth. When I closed my eyes to find my wish, I saw a rush of faces: Finn, his family, Julia, the Morgans, Tyler, Lisa, Mimi, Benjamin, a newborn baby, and finally, me. Following the knowing of my heart, I opened my eyes and blew until all the spores twisted off into the air, floating the way of wishes.

"Well?"

"I can't tell you or it won't come true!"

We had more hiking to do and I walked ahead, my muscles working in ways they never had before.

After we had gone a bit further, Finn asked. "Can I pace you?"

"Pace me?"

"Walk in front of you to slow you down. I can hear you breathing."

"Oh, lead the way." I waved my arm in front of me.

"Don't mind if I do." He blew me a kiss.

After a few minutes my pulse slowed, my chest relaxed and my breathing regulated. He also reminded me to drink water, and all his care lit up my heart with love. Finn might think he didn't see me, but he did.

The sun was high in the sky by the time we made it to the lake. Proud of what we had accomplished, we stood still. The smooth water was like a mirror, reflecting the beauty of the surrounding hills, trees, and sky.

"My family and I used to take dips in this lake," he said.

Sweaty from the hike, I pulled off Lisa's boots and stripped down to my sports bra and underwear.

Finn watched, smiling at me and my body that he'd never seen so much of. "You don't have to do this," he said.

"I'm not doing it just because you can't. I'm doing it for me, too."

The cold water stung my feet, but instead of fighting it, I accepted it, which made going in possible. Once I got deeper, I sank and swam to the center of the lake.

The sweat and dust washed from my skin. My achy muscles relaxed, and my mind followed. I shook my head and let my hair flow loose around me.

As the sun warmed my face, I remembered the hot bath I took at Tyler's. That day, the water had removed a layer of sadness. Today it began to heal me. It was tiny reprieves like this that made letting go a little more bearable.

The past and future weren't mine to hold, not in any real way. Floating in the water, the missing pieces of me didn't have to fit anywhere or even make sense, and with Finn waiting for me at the edge of the lake, it was easy to exist in only what was.

CHAPTER 16

Lisa's pending return weighed time down for me. On top of that, the inevitable expiration date for Finn and me loomed. Days turned into weeks. Finn and I spent time watching movies, talking, hiking, and gazing into each other's eyes.

After a few days of not speaking to Julia, I called to apologize for pushing her away. Before forgiving me she briefly lectured me about how unhealthy my turtling was for our friendship. I promised to do better.

Tyler and I occasionally crossed paths at work and fumbled around each other. When I attempted to make small talk, he found ways to occupy himself and keep his distance. Like a car crash, our friendship was wrecked. It was still unclear if we were salvageable or not.

Finn continued to monitor his family from a safe distance. One night we parked across the street from his house. Through the front, unshaded window we saw his dad sleeping in a La-Z-Boy chair with a laptop resting on his stomach. His mom stared blankly at the TV. A light shone through Violet's bedroom window. Finn's room was dark.

I saw Violet in the halls at school. The happy glint in her eyes hadn't returned. Several times I offered to eat lunch with her, but she'd chosen to hang out with a new group of kids instead. Finn worried about her choice of friends and hated not being able to enforce his big brother duties. He thought she'd pull further away if I tried to intervene, so we crossed our fingers and let her be.

Finally, thirty-six days after Lisa left me her scribbled note, she returned.

We'd just arrived home from one of my late shifts at work to find the house bright when it should've been dark.

"Damn it! Lisa's back. I didn't put the box away."

Finn's energy tingled on my shoulder. "It's all good," he said. "You've been waiting for this."

Lisa's car was in the garage, and I squeezed mine in next to hers. Once parked, I got out of the car and leaned against it trying to calm myself by breathing in and out but failed.

"Let her do all the talking," Finn said. "You've got this, Goodnight."

Lisa opened the door and stood, still, just a black shadow against the kitchen light behind her. "You're home," she said.

"So are you," I said.

She held something in her hand. When I stepped inside the kitchen she backed up, making space for me to enter. The counters were cluttered with full wine bottles and empty glasses. She'd emptied her drinking cabinet.

"You're drinking?" My cheeks burned hot.

Her eyes flashed briefly at me, a look I was used to. Yet, instead of saying something rude she closed her eyes and took a deep breath. When she opened her eyes, her face was calm and unrecognizable. Time had warped and she looked younger, more like she did in the photos. The perpetual blond streaks in her hair had been dyed a one-tone brown. She wore no makeup and the skin around her eyes was a blotchy red.

"I'm dumping it," she said.

"Oh," I said.

She held up her hand. In it was a picture of her with the man I believed was my dad. "So, you know?" she asked.

I felt like I was watching the pivotal scene in a movie, on the edge of my seat, waiting for the plot to shift. "I only know there were two of us and... Sophia's gone."

Her shoulders dropped and her eyes closed briefly, as if hearing the name was too much. "I planned to tell you everything when I got back..."

"You're about eighteen years too late." My voice had risen.

Her eyes shifted away from me. "I am. Eighteen years next week will be the anniversary of their deaths."

Their deaths?

The tiny bit of hope I'd held inside for a living, breathing father escaped with my sigh. *They were both gone.*

"My birthday," I whispered.

Lisa blinked. "It's always been a hard day for me."

I scoffed. "Every day is a hard day for you."

She sighed, looking at the picture in her hand. "You look so much like your dad."

After all this time, this was her first mention of him. She'd kept him from me. Kept them both from me. I snapped, "Wow. It's all a bit surprising considering I didn't even know I had one."

"I understand why you're angry, but I'd like to be able to explain..."

"I've been waiting weeks for an explanation. Oh, wait, let's make that my whole life!"

Possibly seeking a way to escape, Lisa glanced at an unopened bottle on the counter. I leapt forward and grabbed it, throwing it toward the sink. Glass shattered. Red liquid sprayed out around the room.

Lisa gasped. We silently watched the wine drip down the counter, over the cabinet, and onto the floor. Her jeans and shirt were stained with tiny droplets. The smell of alcohol filled the air and I gagged.

She looked from the mess to me. I bristled, waiting for her harsh words, demanding that I clean it up. But they didn't come. Carefully, she stepped around the mess and headed for the door.

Lifting my hands out in front of me, I said, "I'm not sorry I did that."

But I was.

"I can't be near it. I have to change my clothes," she said. Her feet bounding quickly up the stairs were almost enough to muffle the sound of her crying.

I rubbed my temples, not wanting to worry about how she was feeling. Not wanting to be the reason she relapsed, I grabbed the paper towel roll to clean up the mess I'd made.

Tears dripped down my face. Focusing on what I was doing, I tried to filter out the pain of what she had taken from me. I gathered the larger pieces of glass with my hands and used a broom to sweep up the tiny shards. With a soapy sponge, I rubbed unsuccessfully at the blood-red stains on the cabinet.

When I'd finished, I uncorked all five full bottles to varying pops. I'd never opened one before but had seen her do it often. One by one, I tilted them upside down, listening to the evil liquid gurgle into the drain.

The bottles clanged roughly against each other as I threw them into a trash bag. I placed the wine glasses on top of them. The bottle opener landed with a final clank. To overpower the scent, I lit a candle, then grabbed the loops of the trash bag and carried it to the backyard where we kept the bins.

Finn followed me, quiet. The heavy glass bottles bumped against each other until finally settling at the bottom of the can.

I raised my eyes to Finn's. "I shouldn't have done that."

"You have every right to be pissed," he said.

Ready to hear her out, I went back inside. Seeing her now and knowing why she was the way she was didn't take away my anger, but it did make me curious enough to give her space to explain. Whether she'd gone to rehab for her, me or both of us didn't matter. At least it was done.

I followed the sound of sniffles and found Lisa sitting on the kitchen floor with her head in her hands.

When I cleared my throat, she looked up. She had a box of tissues tucked beneath one arm. Part of me was sad for her and the other part didn't want to care. Like a peace offering, she placed the box of tissues in front of her. I sat down on the floor too.

"Thank you for cleaning up." She waved her hand at the kitchen.

I nodded.

"This isn't going to be easy for me," she said.

"I'm overdue for the truth."

"I know," she said.

I'd waited so long, I wanted to reach inside of her and pull everything out of her mouth at once. "Tell me how they died." In childhood, my voice had been silenced and the little girl still inside me spoke up now.

"Are you sure you want me to start there?" Her eyes shone with tears. I imagined they'd been caged in, building up for years.

"Where else would you start?"

"It was all my fault." She shook her head as if some invisible person had disagreed with her statement. "At least, I used to think it was my fault. I've been told I need to see it otherwise. We were in the mountains when it happened. There was still over a month before my due date, and I wanted a quick getaway. The doctor said it would be okay since I wasn't even dilated."

I remained still, not wanting to interrupt what I'd been waiting to hear.

"The labor pains started the night before we were going to come home. They came on fast and were getting closer and closer. The hospital was over an hour away. I wanted to wait for the rain to stop, but Ben said we had to go. I told him it wasn't safe to drive right then, but he said it was fine. That it was time for him to start taking care of his girls."

She rocked herself back and forth while clutching her stomach.

I considered reaching out to touch her but didn't. Then I thought about stopping her, telling her she could tell me the rest later, but then she'd have to start all over.

"I don't remember it all, but suddenly we were sliding onto the wrong side of the road. I tried to hang on for all of us, but there was nothing I could do. The truck behind us screeched as it tried to stop, but it hit our driver's side door. We spun around, and I blacked out."

She continued to rock slowly, her eyes closed. "I was told I was alert enough to deliver you in the ambulance, but I have no memory of it. They said there were complications from there. Sophia was delivered via C-Section at the hospital, but by then she wasn't breathing."

Eyes still closed, she leaned back against the wall and rested her head. "When I woke up the next day Mimi was sitting next to me. I'd never seen her look so sad." Her voice shook first and then her body took over.

Tears dripped from her eyes, and it was then that I recognized the warmth of my own tears on my cheeks.

"I screamed and tried to get up but could barely move from my injuries and the C-section. They gave me a shot of something to calm me and I slept. When I woke up again, Mimi was there holding a baby. She told me that you and I were the only survivors."

She took a deep breath. "It wasn't until days later that I was pressed to finally name you. Ben and I had picked names but hadn't told anyone what they were. We'd decided to name you in alphabetical order. Our firstborn would be Claire, the second Sophia."

She opened her eyes and looked at me in a way she didn't have the courage to do eighteen years ago.

I wiped at my tears and met her gaze.

"I wished that I had died that day, too. From that point on, I did everything I could to forget about what I'd done and all I'd lost."

The first story about a father I'd never known I had was not about the way he'd lived, but about the way he'd died. The truth had been presented swiftly and directly, just the way I'd wanted, but now I wanted to give it back. I didn't want this to be the reason that Lisa had been an apathetic mother.

I didn't want this pain for anyone. The hardness around my heart began to loosen.

To think that she'd carried the guilt for so long made me nauseous. "It's not your fault," I told her.

"I'm trying to believe that," she said.

"Why did you keep it from me?"

"Everything I say will just sound like an excuse."

"Humor me," I said.

"I was young and heartbroken. By the time you were old enough to understand, I didn't think it mattered anymore. I thought you'd be better off not knowing."

"By trying to forget them, you forgot about me, too." My voice was small like my six-year-old self.

"I never forgot though. Every time I looked at you, I remembered. It would've been better if I'd just left you, but I couldn't bring myself to physically leave. I thought staying while Mimi took care of you would be okay."

I couldn't say what would've been better—having her physically gone—or just there as she had been. She'd been in the shadow of a role she couldn't play.

She put her hand at the base of her neck and rubbed her fingers over her skin, leaving marks from the pressure. "I hope one day you'll be able to forgive me."

Forgiving her would be a weight lifted from both of our souls, but I wasn't sure I was ready for the weightlessness of that yet.

"I have more work to do. I have therapy every other day and AA meetings at least once a day—more often if I need that. I know I can't go back and make it better, but I promise to try from now on." She placed her hand over her heart.

"What made you finally go to rehab?"

"Finn," she said.

"Finn?" I asked.

"Well, the loss of Finn. When Eric described his wife, as so lost in her grief, it was as if he was describing me. It was as if Ben was talking to me and asking me to get help. For the first time ever, I felt safe enough to talk about what happened. Hearing it from his perspective made me realize how not dealing with my pain affected others. I felt empathy for him, for her, and finally for me."

Connection after connection clicked, like dominos falling upon each other. Finn's death had led Lisa back to life. Finn's mom had to get lost so mine could be found—it wasn't a fair trade.

"Oh," I said.

Lisa feeling empathy wasn't something I'd ever experienced. I wasn't ready to feel it for her yet and I wasn't sure if I ever could. I had put a wall up between me and Lisa years ago—this wasn't enough to bring it crumbling down.

"How did you meet him?" I asked.

"At a bar. Normally, I'm the one that gets picked up on, but this time, I hit on him. I actually don't think he was there to meet anyone. I'm surprised he even came home with me. It was as if a force outside of us made it happen. Somehow it was meant to be."

I thought about Mimi and how everything seemed linked to her and Finn. Had Mimi been the force?

"Did you know he was married?" I asked.

"It's easier when they're married. I only wanted distraction, not love. Eric is the first man I felt connected to since your dad."

"Did anything happen with the two of you?" I asked.

"I tried to get him drunk to get things going. He wouldn't even let me touch his arm, until you arrived home, and we began talking about Finn. So, no, other than talking and crying on both our parts, nothing happened between us physically," she said.

Receiving confirmation of this was a relief for Finn and his family.

"Good. Well, I don't want you to see him again. His family doesn't deserve to suffer any more than they already have."

"I agree," she said.

"So, overnight you decided to go to rehab?" I asked.

"I told him about my drinking, and he brought it up to me. I knew if I didn't go right away, I wouldn't go. I'm glad I did. And when you're ready, I'd like us to go to therapy together," she said.

Her apathy toward me and her drinking had been her way of coping. I didn't like it, but she'd done the best she could with the heartbreak she'd carried. Intentional or not, her inability to heal herself had in turn broken me. But if I let this painful truth bounce off my armor and not find a place inside me, I would be just like her. It would take much more than this conversation to heal us, but she was sitting before me offering an olive branch that I didn't know I'd been waiting for.

"I can probably do that," I said.

"Thank you," she said. "It's late. Maybe we should get some sleep?"

Placing my left hand behind me to push myself up, I felt pain instantly shoot through my palm. "Ow!"

A piece of shattered glass was stuck in my hand.

"Oh, God," Lisa said.

She stood and reached for my good hand. I couldn't recall one time that she'd purposefully touched me. It seemed impossible that she'd become someone else after such a short time away. I hadn't known her before, and I didn't know her now. I ignored her outstretched hand and stood up on my own.

In the bathroom she turned the water on and directed me to put my hand beneath the faucet. "Can I take it out?" she asked.

I nodded. She removed the shard and set it on the counter, her touch foreign. We watched my blood merge with the water going down the drain.

Finn looked worried.

More for his benefit than Lisa's, I said, "I think it looks worse than it is."

She wrapped a towel tightly around my palm. Then closed the lid of the toilet and told me to sit. "Keep the pressure on it," she said.

For several minutes the whirring of the bathroom fan was the only sound.

"So, you were close to Finn?" She broke the silence.

Unsure how to express how much he still meant to me without acknowledging the actual ghost in the room, I just nodded.

"Oh," she said. "His death must've been very hard for you."

"It was."

"I hope you didn't have to go through it alone," she said.

"I had Julia and Ty—" I stopped myself, not wanting to share too much of myself so soon.

"I'm sorry you lost him."

"Thanks."

"Your dad was the love of my life," she said.

How ironic that each of us losing someone we loved could be a thing that tied us together. "I would love to hear about him sometime."

"I thought talking about his death would mean I had to let him go but it's brought a part of him back to life. I will find a way to share him with you."

I believed her, but the pool of our relationship was still cold, and I wasn't ready to dive right in like she seemed ready to do. This wouldn't be as easy as jumping into the cold lake that day on my hike with Finn.

I peeked into the towel and told her the bleeding had stopped. She found some bandages and ointment under the sink, remnants from Mimi's supply when I was a kid, and completed the first mom thing she'd ever done for me.

CHAPTER 17

My alarm went off the next morning at eleven a.m. My shift started at noon.

"Seriously?" I slammed my hand down on the snooze button.

"You should skip work today," Finn said.

My eyes stung and my palm throbbed, but Tyler would have to scramble to cover my shift. I didn't want to make things even harder on him.

"I need to go in," I said.

"You barely slept, Goodnight," he said.

"Seems to be a theme lately."

Hoping for more of water's cleansing power, I stood in a hot shower, waiting for my conflicting feelings to wash away. Stubborn anger toward Lisa had been my constant companion—more a part of me than she'd ever been. It wasn't going down without a fight.

After the shower, I ran a comb through my hair and pulled it back into a ponytail. I checked under my bandage. A crooked scab line had already begun to form. Our physical bodies healed quickly without conscious thought, while our emotional bodies required awareness and work.

Peeking out into the hallway, I saw that Lisa's door was cracked open. All the awkwardness between us couldn't miraculously change overnight. My instinct to stay away from her hadn't gone. I tiptoed down the stairs, and after grabbing a water bottle and a pack of Pop-Tarts I debated leaving her a note that I was going to work. Still unclear about who she was and what we were, I dropped the pen onto the notepad without making a mark.

I clocked in five minutes late with shaky hands. Being tardy and seeing Tyler's car in the parking lot had twisted up my insides. Holding my bandaged hand before me like a white flag, I approached Tyler, who was working the industrial-sized mixer. He pulled out a large ball of dough and plopped it on the table. Beads of sweat dripped from his temples and his face was flushed.

"Can I help?" I asked.

His expression flickered between surprise and annoyance. "I'm not supposed to be here right now, but Freddy didn't show up this morning." He stopped, his eyes zeroing in on my hand. "Whoa. Are you okay?" For weeks he'd only looked at me sideways but now he met my eyes straight on.

My breath caught in my chest, and I coughed. "Uh, yeah, mostly." I thought about all the things I had yet to process about last night, but he was just asking about my hand. "I cut it on a piece of glass. It's not a big deal, but I don't think I should be on the cook table today."

"Right, of course. We can adjust the assignments. You can work the register."

"Thanks," I said.

These were the most words we'd exchanged since Finn had taken over his body and his lips had been on mine.

"You sure you're okay? You look really beat." He rubbed his forehead with the back of his hand.

"Lisa came back from rehab," I said.

"Tyler!" someone called from the other side of the store.

He sighed. "Can we talk later?"

"Yes, of course." I watched him rush away and smiled, glad to know he still cared about me.

"Order up for Eric Peterson!" a voice called from the cut table.

Finn and I looked at each other.

At the front of the store, I gently placed the pizzas for Finn's family inside a warming pouch as if that small gesture would somehow make things easier for them.

Finn went outside to the parking lot to wait. A few minutes later, he and his dad approached the door together. His dad had sprouted a few more gray hairs.

Feigning surprise when he opened the door, I said. "Mr. Peterson?"

"Hi, Claire. I hoped I would see you."

I raised my eyebrows. "Really?"

"I'm picking up some pizzas," he said.

I turned to the shelf behind me. "Right. One pepperoni and olive and one ham and pineapple." I lifted the lids and showed him the pizzas. "That'll be $20.38."

He pulled a twenty and a five from his wallet, and after handing him the change, I asked, "How are you doing?"

"We could be better. How's your mom?"

"Um, she's good. She went to rehab." I kept my voice low. "She's back now, though."

"So, she went after all." He smiled. "I'm glad. She really helped me feel less alone."

I nodded.

"Did you and Lisa talk about everything?" he asked.

"We did." I cringed, knowing that he'd learned about my dad and sister before I had.

"I'm glad she told you. It couldn't have been easy for her," he said.

"I would've preferred to have known all along, but yeah." I shrugged.

"Hey, can you ask about my mom?" Finn asked.

"So, how are Violet and Mrs. Peterson doing?" I asked.

"Mostly the same. I was hoping to get back to our usual routines, hence the pizzas."

The door beeped, signaling a new customer—a woman with two young kids. The kids rushed to the Pac-Man machine. Eric picked up his food and stepped aside.

I said, "I hope it helps, truly. Take care." Then I turned to the woman. "Hi. How can I help you?"

Out of the corner of my eye, I watched Finn follow his dad outside, and—unseen—wave goodbye as he drove away.

Later, on my break, I ate slightly burnt breadsticks that were going to be tossed. Finn sat with me, but there were too many people around to talk and I was tired.

"I wish I could get you a coffee or something," Finn said.

My eyes fluttered, wanting to close. Smiling at him, I rested my chin on my hand. Then, as if Finn's desire had manifested it, Tyler placed a cup of coffee in front of me.

Finn nodded approvingly. "It's time to fix things with him."

Tyler buying a coffee for me was a good sign. "You're a lifesaver." I took a small sip of the warm drink. "You remembered, even down to the almond milk." I looked at the printed sticker on the cup.

He nodded and sat down next to me. "So, Lisa's back?"

"She is."

"Is everything okay?"

"Mostly, I think."

Wanting to keep Tyler with me, but unsure of what to say, I looked to the space across from me to seek guidance from Finn. He was gone.

I turned back to Tyler. "Are you okay?"

His eyes met mine only briefly. "I've been better." He picked at a loose piece of skin on his thumb. "Weren't we talking about you though?" There was a slight smirk on his face.

"My stuff is heavy, and I haven't told Julia yet."

"We don't have to talk about it then," he said quickly.

"No, that's not what I meant. You're my friend too."

He muttered something under his breath that I didn't catch.

"Tyler, can we talk about what happened?"

He stood up. "I think you should go home and get some sleep. We've slowed down and can cover the rest of your shift now."

He had done the thing I noticed most guys do—change the subject when hard topics came up. Maybe it wasn't just a guy thing, though. I bet I did it too. "Are you trying to get rid of me?"

"Claire, you look exhausted," he said.

"I can stay. I don't want to leave you short."

"We'll be fine."

I couldn't leave without trying to salvage us. My feet pressed into the floor, like they were encased in cement.

"I'll go home, but I want to talk about what happened. Not here and now. And not wearing these uniforms. But in clothes, of course." I laughed nervously.

Tyler raised his eyebrows at me and seemed to hide a smile.

"I want to resume our Sunday night dinners." I wasn't asking—I was reclaiming.

He shifted his hat on his head and sighed. "Uh, sure, okay. I'll look at the schedule and make next week work."

Relieved, I said, "Let's go somewhere other than the food court."

"How about the Mexican place down the street?" he asked.

"My favorite," I said.

"I know," he said. "Oh, and it'll be my treat—by then it will be a belated birthday present."

My eyes widened. "You remembered?"

"I know it's coming up. I have it in my phone calendar, so that helped." He smiled.

My stomach fluttered at the fullness of his smile. Sometimes you don't realize how much you miss someone until you feel them returning to you.

"Alright, now get out of here." He walked over to check stock on the cook table.

When I turned Finn was beside me.

"Hey," he said.

The butterflies inside me bounced into each other—confused.

"Yes, I heard and yes I'm a tiny bit jealous, but I want you to go," he said. "Without me."

"Why?"

"You don't need me hanging around all the time. Besides, it's my fault you're in this mess anyway. My being there will make cleaning it up even harder."

"How gentlemanly of you," I said.

"I try," Finn said.

"You succeed."

Once we were outside and out of sight, Finn stopped me. He put his hand on my cheek. I leaned into his energy and closed my eyes.

"Can you still feel me?" he asked.

"Of course I can."

He sighed, then asked in a rush, "Goodnight, will you go to prom with me?"

"Prom? It's two months away. Do we have that long?" I asked.

"Not the real prom, but one of our own. Under your willow tree, maybe?"

"That sounds like my kind of prom. Though I totally would have gone to the real prom with you, too."

"If I was still *here* here I would've taken you. I would've held you in my arms all night. Maybe we would've danced, too," he said, laughing.

I imagined Finn and me dressed up all fancy-like, dancing closely to all the slow songs. "I'll buy a dress and some decorations," I said. "When are we doing this?"

"Soon. How about next Saturday?" Finn asked.

The way he said *soon* made my heart stop. "Is there something you aren't telling me?"

"We might be getting close."

"Oh," I said.

The world around me began to spin. Change was everywhere. It was in the new pink flowers blooming on the trees, in my relationship with Lisa, and in my heart.

Finn said, "Even though my love-giving capacity for you is limited by time, it doesn't make it any less real. I would stay forever if I were still alive. The way I am now, I would only hold you back."

I leaned into him further, soaking up his love. Somehow, I'd become the conclusion to Finn's story, while he'd end up being only a few chapters in mine. Like a blinking cursor at the mercy of a writer, we had no choice but to wait for our final sentence.

CHAPTER 18

On the drive home, I wondered if I'd find the new Lisa who made eye contact or the old Lisa with the half-gone gaze. It was New Lisa, sitting at the kitchen table, wine-glass free. A rainbow of colored envelopes were spread out before her.

"Oh." She bit her lip and looked from me to the light blue envelope in her hand.

My desire to remain under the radar prodded me to get out of her sight. I headed toward the stairs.

Her voice pulled me back.

"I'm leaving for a meeting in a few minutes. I was going to wait on this, but since you're here, can you sit with me?" She reached out her arms, pulling in the envelopes like she was collecting leaves on the lawn.

Finn followed me to the table, and we sat looking at Lisa. I held my breath, preparing myself for more surprises.

"How's your hand?" she asked.

"Fine," I said.

"I brought the mail in this morning, and this was in it." She waved one of the envelopes.

"Is it for me?" I asked, leaning forward.

"It is," she said. "Actually, all of these are for you."

I raised my eyebrows.

"They come every year."

"Why didn't you give them to me?"

"I asked Mimi not to." She flipped through the thick stack of cards in her hand.

I'd madly searched Mimi's desk for answers and hadn't seen these. The empty shoebox on the table gave away the hiding place for secret envelopes. Digging into shoeboxes for answers wasn't something I'd considered.

"Stealing mail is a federal offense, isn't it?"

"Uh, I guess it is," she said. "God, you must hate me."

I ignored that. "Who are they from?"

"They're from Ben's mom. Your grandma."

My face heated up. I remembered asking Mimi about family after meeting Julia's extended family at a party once. She had replied that Lisa was her only child. The sad look in her eyes pushed me from prodding her further. I hadn't even thought to specifically ask about another set of grandparents.

Gripping the table, I spat, "Not only were you unwilling to love me, but you also refused to let anyone else love me. What is wrong with you?"

Instead of turning away from me, she turned toward me. "A lot was wrong with me. I couldn't face any of it. You deserved better."

"Of course I did. Give them to me. Now." I stood, wanting to claw at her like a cat and knock them away from her, leaving scratches on her arms.

"I want you to have them. Please take them."

"How kind of you."

She placed them in my open hands. My name was written in flowery cursive. The return label listed an address in San Diego, CA.

"They're only two hours away? They've been this close all along?"

She put her head down. "I couldn't face them."

A scream hung in my throat, begging to be released. "After they lost their son, you decided to keep me from them, too?"

"I didn't see it that way...at the time. If it helps, I do see now how much I screwed up," she said.

The ease with which this whole new Lisa accepted blame came at me like a slap to my face, unexpected and painful. My anger hit a wall. It was as if she was okay being a punching bag—all take, no fight.

I snarled, "No matter what you say, you can't change the fact that you've ruined my life!" My voice caught between a scream and a sob.

Clutching the envelopes to my chest, I took the stairs two at a time. I slammed my bedroom door, opened it, then slammed it again. "This is so shitty!"

"A thousand percent shitty," Finn said. "But you have family, Goodnight."

"But I've lost so much time with them. It's not fair!"

There was a soft knock at the door. I jumped. "What?" I yelled out.

"Can we talk about this when I get back?" Lisa asked through the door.

"I don't think there is anything more to say," I said.

"I'm so sorry, Claire," she said.

The doorknob jiggled and I leapt forward to lock it. "Leave me alone!" I pushed the angry tears off my cheeks.

After she drove away, Finn sat with me while I sorted the cards by postdate. Oldest on top, newest at the bottom. Every March for the last eighteen years a card addressed to me had been postmarked with plenty of time to arrive by my birthday. I ran my fingers over her handwriting.

The fancy cursive writing on the envelopes was also on the cards within. They all began with the same greeting and closing. Money was folded inside each card, a dollar for how old I had turned that year.

Dearest Claire,

I hope this card finds you well and happy today on your 10th birthday! I have special news to share! You have a new baby cousin! His name is Benny, after your dad. I'm including a picture of him. He's a pudgy little guy and we love him so much. Your Mimi sent us your school picture and the drawing of your willow tree. I put your drawing in a frame and it's hanging in my front room. I show it off to everyone who comes over. You're an amazing artist!

Love always, Grammy and Grampy

I held the wallet-size picture of a baby between my fingers. "I have a cousin."

"So, he would be ... what, about eight years old now?" Finn asked.

"That sounds about right. Mimi sent her pictures of me. I bet she felt guilty keeping me away from them."

The card from this year listed her phone number in the bottom corner.

Dearest Claire,

What a big year this is for you! Happy 18th birthday! I hope all is well with you and your family. It's been so long since we've heard anything from Mimi. If you receive this, please get in touch with me and let me know you're okay. We love you, dear.

Love always, Grammy and Grampy

By the time I'd read the last card, I had three cousins and one hundred and seventy-one dollars.

She'd waited for me for so long and I couldn't wait for her another second. I pulled my phone out and clicked the numbers on the screen.

First ring.

"I'm not sure what to say." I paced.

Second ring. I debated hanging up.

"You'll figure it out," Finn said.

Third ring. My heart pounded.

"Hello?"

"Hello, hi. Can I, uh, speak with Sarah Davis?" I asked.

"Speaking."

"Oh, hi, this is Claire. Claire Goodnight."

There was a sharp intake of breath on the other line. "Claire?"

"Yes. I'm sorry you're only now hearing from me. I literally just found out that you existed and opened all of the birthday cards you sent me. Thank you so much."

"Claire? Is it really you?"

"Yes, it's really me."

"Gabriel, it's Claire! It's *Claire!*" she called out, then to me she said, "Oh, he's outside and can't hear me. Gosh, I'm so glad you called. I hope you know how much we've wanted you in our lives."

"I can tell by the cards."

"Good! I had a feeling you didn't know about us. There are so many people who will be excited to meet you."

"I only recently learned about my dad and sister, too. Like, very recently…"

"You must be so overwhelmed, honey."

"I am," I said.

"I wasn't sure if I'd ever hear from you."

"Mimi passed away—that's why you haven't heard anything from her," I said.

"Oh, I'm so sorry, dear."

"And Lisa is newly back from rehab. Trying to make amends." I rolled my eyes at Finn.

"Oh, goodness. I'm glad she got some help. Do you need anything?"

"No, I'm doing okay," I said.

"We can help with anything. And, Claire, we would love to see you, to finally meet you! We can come to you, or you can come here. Whatever works best for you."

I thought about my prom with Finn and my upcoming dinner with Tyler. My grandmother wasn't going anywhere, but soon Finn would be.

"Maybe in a couple of weeks? I can get the weekend off work and come see you then?"

"That sounds perfect. I hope you and your mom are okay?"

"We're a work in progress," I said. "You must be so angry with her."

"I was, dear, but I forgave her years ago. Thankfully, your Mimi shared things about you with us. That helped. I hoped one day you would learn about us…"

"I'm angry," I said.

"I can see why you would be. Especially if you're just finding out about Ben. Of course, I knew Lisa before the accident. After the shock of the pregnancy wore off, she and Ben were so excited to be parents. She had such a big heart and loved our Benny so much. Hopefully, she can find herself again."

On a whim, I asked her if she knew where my dad and Sophia were buried. It wasn't shocking to learn that they were in the local cemetery. The same one where Finn and Mimi were. All along they'd been so close.

I gave her my cell phone number and I told her I'd call her soon.

"It will be a homecoming and birthday party of sorts," she said.

"I'm not much for big gatherings," I said.

"Ah, your dad wasn't either. Let's see, there is me, your grandpa, your uncle, his wife and their three kids. Would that be okay?" she asked.

"Yes. I can't wait."

"Perfect. If you need anything, please call. And happy early birthday!"

"Thank you…"

"Call me Grammy Sarah, please."

"Thank you, Grammy Sarah."

I hung up the phone and jumped up and down. I had a family. Finn jumped up and down with me.

It was possible to be loved just for being born, after all.

CHAPTER 19

"Happy birthday, C!" Via FaceTime, Julia's bellow and smile stretched across the many miles between us.

It was morning and Finn's smile was brighter than the sun that slanted like liquid gold through my blinds. "I thought for sure I'd be the first." He shrugged. "Happy birthday, Goodnight. I love you."

"Thank you." My response intended for both of them.

"Did I wake you up?" Julia asked.

"Sort of," I said. "How'd the meeting go yesterday?"

Julia had joined an LGBTQ+ club at school to meet new people. We hadn't been interested in joining clubs before—our two-person club had been enough—but though she hadn't said much, I knew it was hard on her not knowing anyone at her new school. While she'd been loyal to me, being a loner like me wasn't her thing.

"We painted signs for the upcoming 5K we're doing. You'll never guess what happened after, though." She ran her fingers through her long black hair, a faraway look in her eyes.

"You know I won't be able to guess! Unless...oh, does it have something to do with the infamous Tanya?"

"She kissed me!"

"OMG, J! How was your first kiss?"

"It took my breath away. Just like you said your kiss with..."

"J, it's okay to talk about him. I'm so freaking happy for you," I said.

I'd come to realize that Julia had been holding back on sharing details about her new life, wanting to protect me, so the day I'd spilled the news about Lisa and my extended family I'd begged her to talk about herself. I told her no matter what my life looked like, I always wanted to know the truth about hers. I knew this made me a hypocrite since I'd kept Finn from her, but I wanted to be a constant for her like she was for me.

"When do I get to meet her?" I asked.

"We'll do a FaceTime call with her soon, I promise."

We hung up to get ready for school. Taking more time than usual, I straightened my hair and put on a little makeup. I chose a light green shirt, jeans, and a black cardigan, instead of my usual black hoodie. There was no one at school to impress and Tyler had given me the day off at work, so the extra little bits were for me and Finn.

I walked out of the bathroom.

"You're so hot," Finn said. He pressed his ghostly lips to mine.

A warm, buttery aroma that instantly reminded me of Mimi floated up the stairs. I crinkled my brows.

"What's the matter?" Finn asked.

"It smells like Mimi's baking," I said.

My stomach growled and my heart lifted a little. Ever since Lisa's return, I'd dreaded this morning, knowing that for her this day had never been about celebrating. Rehab and her numerous therapy sessions and meetings continued to keep her darkness away. Her perpetually closed arms had remained open since the day she returned. My flight response around her had begun to subside.

As my foot hit the bottom step I heard Lisa whisper, "She's coming."

Finn rushed down ahead of me. I took a deep breath and turned the corner to the kitchen.

Several plates of chocolate chip muffins sat on the kitchen counter, a single pink candle sticking out of each one. An iPad was propped up on some of Mimi's old books and Julia and her family were on the screen. Lisa lit the last candle, then looked up at me, a closed-mouthed smile on her face.

"Okay, go!" Julia said. She, her family, Lisa, and Finn erupted into the Happy Birthday song.

I looked from the screen to Lisa and Finn. My birthday mornings of years past had encompassed Mimi quietly singing to me and my favorite chocolate chip muffins. The days were like a dark secret we kept from Lisa. Mimi was missing, but Lisa was there, singing. Her hands held her up against the counter.

"Make a wish!" Mrs. Morgan called out from the screen. I closed my eyes and repeated the wish from the dandelion field. After several attempts I blew out all eighteen candles, receiving cheers and applause once the flames were out.

I took a bite of a muffin. The chocolate melted onto my lips—warm, gooey, and familiar. Gray clouds had always hovered over my birthday. Mimi and I had escaped the doom at our house by joining the Morgans for dinner and cake at theirs. Julia's family merging with Lisa was unexpected and surprisingly pleasant.

We chatted for a few minutes until the Morgans had to go about their lives.

After we hung up, I looked at Lisa. "Mimi would be proud of you."

Mimi had probably hoped for all of this between me and Lisa from up there wherever she was.

Lisa put a hand on her chest and closed her eyes. She'd been doing that a lot since returning home.

"Ben and Sophia probably would be, too," she said.

I sucked in my breath and looked away from her. The day was never about me for her.

Finn placed his hand over mine. "Breathe," he whispered.

"But you're the one who matters most," she said.

Finally. The words landed in the center of my heart, right where I needed them.

"I'm proud of you, too," I said The words sounded smoother coming out than I felt saying them.

"Is it okay if I take you out to dinner tonight?" she asked.

"Sure," I said.

"Maybe she can help you pick out a dress for our prom," Finn said.

I rolled my eyes at him, but he insisted. It was a push from both him and Mimi, I was sure.

"I need to pick up a dress at the mall. Will you come with me?"

"Yes, of course." She attempted to hide a smile by quickly turning away, but I saw it.

Concentrating at school that day was nearly impossible. All I could think about was my plan to go to the cemetery that afternoon, feeling oddly nervous to be near a part of them that still existed on earth, even if it was six feet underground. I'd been thinking about visiting the cemetery ever since my conversation with Grammy Sarah. Today seemed like an appropriate day to do it.

Inside the stately iron gates, the old-fashioned upright headstones appeared. Their elaborate stone engravings of names and dates were faded and stained with age. It didn't seem possible that anyone visited these century-old graves, but still they remained, forever holding a place for the long gone.

Finn sat beside me, silent, watching the rows of the dead slide by the window. I wondered how many of them had lived the lives they wanted. If they had said and done all the things they'd planned to do. Had some of them remained behind, like Finn, seeking to finish what was left undone?

It would take hours of searching to locate their headstones on my own. We stopped at the cemetery office. When I pulled open the wooden door, the smell of dust and an emotion I couldn't quite define rushed forward on the air-conditioned breeze.

"How can I help you?" A man stood up from a desk piled high with manila envelopes and loose scraps of paper. He pushed his glasses from his face up to the top of his head.

"I'm not sure of the last names used for the graves I'm looking for. Benjamin and Sophia are their first names. The last name could be Davis or possibly Goodnight."

He picked up a pencil and a Post-It pad. He shifted his glasses back to his nose and scribbled down the names. "Do you know when they were buried?"

"It would've been about eighteen years ago. Almost to the day." I shifted my feet and rubbed my sweaty palms against my pants.

"Those should be in our system. Just a moment, miss," he said. His chair creaked as he sat down, his fingers clicking on the keyboard.

"This feels like coming home." Finn pretended to play the drums, ba dah bum as one does after telling a bad joke.

I rolled my eyes at him.

The man returned with a map and a black Sharpie. "Okay, miss. They're both under the name of Davis. And finding them will be easy peasy—they share a plot."

"They were buried in the same coffin?" My heart fluttered. I imagined my tiny baby sister cocooned in a blanket and gently tucked into the crook of our dad's arm.

He nodded. "It's fairly rare, but it makes sense. Your Sophia was so young, and they died on the same day."

Your Sophia.

He'd said it like she was mine, which made it feel truer than before.

"It's perfect, actually," I said. "I just didn't know it was possible."

His eyes shone through his glasses. "It is lovely, isn't it? So, we are here, and you want to go here." He marked a section near the back of the cemetery with a star. "Just follow the road right out front and you'll find it."

I thanked him and clutched the shiny paper. A treasure map that would take me to a part of me that I never knew existed and was finally about to find.

Back in the car, I said, "Sophia got my dad's last name, and I got Lisa's."

"Maybe it was meant to be a tribute to him?"

When I glanced over at him with a slight eye roll, he said, "Come on, the devil's advocate is kind of my role, right?"

I smiled half-heartedly. "You're right though. I like the way you think. I'm glad they used his name."

"I'm just over that hill that way." He pointed out the window.

"I know."

"How?"

"Have I not told you I went to your grave a few times?"

"No, but that's sweet," he said.

"More like torturous. You know it lists *Loving son, brother, and friend*?"

"Yeah."

"You were so much more than that. How can the entirety of a person be described in just four words? It's not enough."

"There's a limited amount of space," Finn pointed out.

"Ugh, devil's advocate, huh?" I sighed.

"I do understand what you mean though. What would you add about me?"

"Something about how the depth of your soul is reflected in your eyes. Something about the way you make me feel when you look at me. Something about your happy dance and how much you loved basketball..."

"Yeah, that definitely wouldn't fit, but I love that you think those things." He placed his hand on my leg.

"I know it's not possible to write up all that on a gravestone. It's just always bothered me that in death, a life is taken down to the bare minimum. People are way more than the role they played relationally to others. If someone walked by and saw your grave who didn't know you, they wouldn't know how great you were."

"But they didn't know me, so they weren't supposed to know. What I was to those who knew me is in their heart, not on that rock."

"It just doesn't feel like enough."

"No matter what it says, I'd still be gone, and it doesn't bother me. I know what I meant to people."

"You didn't really know what you meant to me. Not when you were alive."

"You're right, but that's why I'm still here," he said.

"Not everyone gets to come back as a ghost to really know."

"Maybe you don't have to be a ghost to know. Maybe you just know. I'm here more for you than I am for me. Goodnight, you wishing that you could mark a gravestone with how much you loved someone is an awesome idea, just not one that would fit with the way the whole funeral world is set up—you know?"

I nodded. Maybe those left behind filled in the missing gaps within their hearts. That would have to be enough. I soaked in the energy flowing between us, grateful that he was there for me.

Glancing down at the map, then up at the markers at the edge of the road, I noticed we were in the right section. I pulled over.

"You ready?" he asked.

Wanting to "meet" my family alone, I said, "I am. Do you mind if I go alone?"

"Of course not."

I stepped out onto the grass, knowing that they had to be close based on the map. Moving slowly, I read the names.

My eyes landed on their headstone.

The brown stone was split in two by a beige line embedded between their names. Below the dates, it said *Gone Too Soon*. And how my heart both ached and lifted to see *Son, Father, Fiancé, Friend* and *Daughter, Sister*. The world, or anyone who walked by here, would know they'd meant something to someone. They were so much more than those titles, but it made sense now—it was all for those left behind.

Daughter: she belonged to the two people who created her. Sister: for nearly nine months Sophia and I had shared everything. Our noses likely smushed against each other's, our hands swinging umbilical cords like tiny jump ropes. Father: half of him made two people and for that alone, he deserved this title. He would've heard our heartbeats at doctor's appointments and held his hand to Lisa's belly to feel our kicks. He would've already loved us. I knew it.

As Finn had said, my heart's job was to fill in the gaps left by the basic descriptions—that weren't basic at all, not really.

I traced the letters of their names, the stone cold and rough on my skin. I couldn't remember a time when I hadn't felt like something was missing from my life. The lonely ache—the half-completeness—had festered in my cells, drifted through my blood, and grown into my bones. My dad and Sophia were an answer to a question I hadn't known I was asking. They were the missing pieces.

My mind replayed the accident. The swerving, the truck, and the final crash against the tree. In that instant, the path to our happy little family of four hit a dead end. Two lives were subtracted from the equation and we, the remainders, were flung away, unprepared for the new terrain. Grief was a slow and painful stitching together of what life was without.

Lisa had put her healing on hold, and I'd never had a chance to try.

A seed of unlovability had been planted inside of me the moment Lisa chose to deny our new reality. Roots took hold, wrapped around my heart, and were watered by Lisa's neglect. Without tools, I couldn't weed out the ugly thing forming at the center of me.

I'd been stuck in run mode my whole life but running away from Lisa wouldn't save me. That damn growth would go with me wherever I went. Now I knew that her inability to love me had nothing to do with me and everything to do with her.

It was then that I realized what the unknown emotion in the air of the cemetery office was.

Acceptance.

Acceptance of everything that couldn't be changed.

And peace.

After several quiet minutes of trying to feel them, I gave up. It would be crazy to think they'd been hanging around a cemetery all these years, waiting for me.

The spirits of those we lost were inside us, beside us—they were like ghosts we carried—unlike Finn who magically appeared for me. Looking for my dad and sister outside of myself wasn't the way—I needed to look within.

I located Finn lying on top of his grave. His arms were tucked behind his head, his feet crossed over each other. He was like a poem; clear, confusing, and breathtaking all at once. How bittersweet it was that one day I would no longer see him and instead have to seek him in my heart.

CHAPTER 20

When we arrived home and found the house was still wine glass free, I released a breath of relief. Today was the test, the anniversary of the worst day of her life.

I blinked a few times to be sure that Lisa, in a pretzel-like yoga pose on the floor, wasn't a hallucination. Holding her back up straight, she smiled and asked where I wanted to go for dinner. She nodded her approval at my choice of an Italian restaurant near the mall, then shifted her position.

Lisa showered while I did homework. By the time we pulled up to the restaurant, the sun was setting. The sky like a canvas splashed with oranges, pinks, and purples. A painting across the sky that would disappear before it could fully be interpreted.

Before we walked inside, Finn told me he wasn't coming in. I stepped back from Lisa and told her to go in without me, that I'd be right there.

After Lisa had gone inside, I asked, "Did you wait to tell me so I wouldn't argue with you?"

"Maybe…"

"What will you do?"

"Don't worry about me, Goodnight. I just want you two to connect. Alone." His eyes were steady on mine.

"I can tell I'm not going to be able to change your mind," I said. "Will you take a birthday selfie with me and the sunset before you go?"

"I won't show up!"

"But I'll always know you were with me." I pulled my phone from my back pocket. "Come on, before it gets too dark."

Finn put his arm around me, and I tilted my head against his cheek. He was right—only my reflection appeared on the screen—but I snapped away anyway, positioning us with the sun behind us.

"Okay, now a silly one," I said.

"How about a kissing one?" Finn asked.

We puckered our lips. I clicked some more.

"Are they post-worthy?" he asked.

The only place they'd be posted was in my heart, or in a frame in my room. Yet when I scrolled through them, I noticed a slight blur—a rainbow-like light—near my cheek where Finn's presence had been.

Maybe one day, I would be able to look back on the pictures and see a part of him too.

"You're more beautiful than any sunset I've ever seen," he said.

"Ditto," I said.

"You think I'm beautiful?" He posed, his hands on his hips.

"Duh!"

"I'll find you after you get your dress. I want to be surprised."

I watched Finn disappear around the corner, feeling a piece of me leave with him. After he was really gone, I wondered if I would sense him like a phantom limb.

Inside the restaurant, a man with slicked-back hair and a black, button-up shirt stood behind a small podium. He asked if I was meeting someone. I nodded.

The restaurant was dimly lit. A few scattered couples sat at small rectangular tables with lit candles as centerpieces. The walls were a deep red that matched the carpet.

Lisa sat at a table near the back looking at a menu. I'd never been to this little eatery but had overheard conversations at school about it being a good date spot. Tonight might've been a way for me to have a date of sorts with Finn, but he'd had different ideas.

"I'm with her." I pointed to Lisa.

"Oh, yes." He grabbed a menu and led me to the table. When I pulled out my seat, he asked. "You must be sisters?"

I remained silent, wondering if she would claim me or not.

After a brief pause, Lisa spoke up. "Actually, this is my daughter."

The word daughter floated between us. To the outside world, we looked like we belonged together, but to me, we didn't quite fit. Not yet.

He glanced back and forth between us. "You must get that a lot?"

The angry little girl inside me kept quiet. It wasn't possible to appease her after only a few days. I opened the menu and said, "Nope, this is a first."

He cleared his throat, stepped a few feet away, and returned with an open wine bottle.

"Would you care for some house wine?" He tipped the bottle over Lisa's glass.

My hand shot forward, covering the top of it.

Lisa lifted my hand away. "No, I'm fine, thanks. We won't be needing these," she said.

"No problem." He picked the glasses up by their stems. "I'll give you a few minutes to look over the menu."

We reviewed the food options in silence, resetting ourselves before speaking. We both ordered beef ravioli with side salads.

"I went to the cemetery today," I said.

At the same time, she said. "I found a therapist for us. Are you still okay going with me?"

We nervously laughed. Then waited for the other to respond. When I didn't speak, she did.

"I thought this day was supposed to be about you?" she asked.

"Seeing their graves was about me," I said.

"I was still in the hospital on the day of the funerals. I've never visited."

"It says fiancé on his gravestone."

"Oh." She busied herself with the napkin in her lap. "It was good of them to include that."

"I thought so, too," I said.

"Do you feel better for having gone?"

"I feel more complete, if that makes sense."

"It does. Maybe we can go together next time."

I nodded, then sipped my drink. "I'd like to hyphenate my name to Goodnight-Davis." The idea had come to me on the drive to the restaurant. It felt right, perfect in fact.

She choked on her water. "Okay," she said.

I didn't need her approval or for her to cosign—I could do it on my own; I'd just wanted her to know. "Why didn't you give me his last name in the first place?" I asked.

"I couldn't wait to have his last name. But I realized I never would. Maybe that's why, in my medicated haze, I chose not to give it to you. Fewer reminders, less to explain."

I would've known to ask questions if we'd had different last names. But she probably hadn't thought that far ahead.

"Sophia's death certificate listed Goodnight. It was nice to see they gave her his name on her headstone though," I said.

"I'm glad they did that. Looking back, it's terrible that I didn't list him on paper as your dad. I barely even remember making that decision, what with all the drugs, shock, and sadness."

"Okay," I said.

She could've changed it later when she wasn't drugged but hadn't. Being mad about that didn't change it.

Acceptance.

I thought about Lisa's therapy question. Finn would tell me to go, Mimi would want me to go. I bet dad and Sophia would, too. I wasn't sure about it, but they deserved it, so for them I would try. For me, too.

"I'll go to therapy with you," I said.

"I appreciate you giving me a chance to make this better."

"You won't be able to make anything better, but I think we can move forward, differently," I said.

"I know I can't undo the past, but I do want to be a part of your life, for real," she said.

The candlelight flickered off the water glasses and I remembered the candles on the muffins that morning. She'd have to keep showing up for me if she wanted me to make space in my heart for her.

After dinner we walked through the mall and Lisa asked, "What do you need a dress for?"

A stomach full of ravioli wasn't the best state for dress shopping, but I worked the rest of the week and wouldn't have another chance to go.

"Um, it's a prom dress, but I'm not going to the prom," I said.

"Oh," she said.

"Which reminds me, would you mind not being home on Saturday night?" I asked.

"Do you have a date?" she asked.

"I'd rather not talk about it. I just need the house." I looked at her, hard, ending the subject with my eyes.

She didn't have the right to ask more questions or demand answers, not yet. She might've given me the title of daughter to a stranger, but I wasn't ready to award her with the role of mother yet.

"Of course," she said. "I'll find a place to stay."

Lisa followed me around a party store, looking at her phone. I bought a small disco ball and several strings of white lights. They required electricity, so I'd have to plug them into an extension cord. We could use my cell phone for music.

Lisa trailed behind me at the department store, until I finally asked her for advice. She brought several dresses into the dressing room for me. I changed alone. I couldn't recall one time that I'd undressed in front of her. When I needed help with zippers, I opened the door slightly and asked for assistance with my back to her.

All the dresses were beautiful—for other people. Most of them were itchy and didn't match my personality. Until the last one. It was a full-length black dress with spaghetti straps. It was simple with a bit of sparkle on the bodice and a flared skirt.

Lisa found me a pair of silver strappy heels to match. I piled my hair on top of my head and took a turn before the mirror. I imagined Finn's expression the moment he'd see me in it and butterflies flitted inside me.

As we drove home, I said, "Thank you for making this day about me."

She put her hand on mine and squeezed it for several long seconds. I wanted to pull away, but I didn't.

CHAPTER 21

The weekend arrived quickly, which was good and bad. Each moment with Finn was sacred and I wanted to slow time down, but we were both excited for that night.

Setting up for my own personal prom wasn't something I'd ever imagined doing, and it wasn't easy on my own. After almost an hour of tossing a string of lights through branches, I was finally able to twist the remainder around the tree trunk. I'd hung the disco ball from a limb above our grass dance floor.

Even though it wasn't quite dark when I plugged it all in, the tree twinkled like a clear night filled with stars.

I rubbed my moist forehead with the back of my arm and called, "Finn!"

He walked around from the side yard. "It's perfect. I wish I could be the one surprising you."

"You being here is more than enough," I said.

"Are you ready for our prom?" he asked.

I looked down at what I was wearing and laughed. "Not quite."

"Girl, we don't have time to waste. Go and get dressed!" he said.

Being reminded of our ticking time bomb made me want to shrivel up and cry. We may not have had a ghost handbook, but we both knew he couldn't stay forever. His leaving felt imminent, and I hated not knowing how or when he'd go. Yet crying about it would only waste our time. All we had was now. I'd make it count.

"Be prepared to be blown away by my beauty," I said.

"It's too late for that."

"Aw, Finn. I was going to say that if you hadn't already been in love with me, you would've been after tonight."

"I like my odds," he said.

Once again, I used the shower to cleanse my soul. The stream of water rinsed away the unknowns with Lisa, my unopened college letters that I'd been ignoring, and my upcoming dinner with Tyler. Those things weren't going anywhere, but Finn was.

I dried and curled my hair, then pulled half of it up into a clip, letting the long curls fall loose around my shoulders.

In Lisa's bathroom, I found a silver eye shadow. Along with that, I applied extra blush, eyeliner, and heavy mascara.

When I stood before the mirror in my black dress and silver shoes, I barely recognized myself. It was me and not me. Now that I was aware of Sophia, I wondered if parts of her had always shown through me like they did right now.

Minutes later, I walked beneath the willow, into our space, accessible only to us.

Finn stood with both hands clasped behind his back. His unconventional forever outfit of jeans and sweatshirt was made perfect by the diamond light shimmering through him like fireflies. His grin broadened as his eyes drifted from my hair slowly down to my feet.

I spun in my dress, the slick material flowing out around me, free. Finn didn't speak.

"It's impossible for me to take your breath away," I moved toward him.

He cleared his throat. "I thought it was impossible for you to be more beautiful than beautiful," he said.

"Thank you, Finn," I said. His compliment brought a swift flush through me that made it all the way to my heart.

"I feel so underdressed." He looked down at his eternal outfit, then pretended to tighten a bow tie.

I laughed. "It's been a lifelong dream of mine to go to prom with you. You could've been nude, and I might still be excited about it!"

"Ha ha." He eyed me with heat in his eyes. "If only you knew how badly I want to touch you right now."

My cheeks flushed hotter. "I do know because I feel the same way."

We'd made a playlist together earlier in the week, picking a mixture of dance and slow songs. I pressed shuffle on my music app and set my phone on the lounge chair. A slow song melodically drifted through the air between us, pulling us closer.

"Aren't you going to ask me to dance?" I asked.

Holding an upturned hand out to me, he bowed slightly. "Goodnight, will you dance with me for as long as we both shall live?"

My breath caught in my throat. I placed my hand in the air of his hand and whispered, "I would dance with you forever."

His energetic current met mine and we swayed together without speaking. Even when the pop songs played, we remained close and quiet.

Finn broke the silence first. "Do you believe in past lives?" he asked.

I pulled away from him slightly to look up at his face. Even though for much of our school years we didn't speak, I'd always felt like I'd known him on a deeper, unspoken level. "I think so. Why?"

"I don't know much about them, but it feels like I've always known you."

"I feel that way too," I said.

"I will find you in another life," he promised.

"One day we'll get our timing right."

He nodded. "I'll do everything in my power to make that happen."

A cascade of tears threatened to fall, but I held them off. While the conversation partly felt like a goodbye, this wasn't the time for an ugly cry. I would save that for later.

"Has me being here this way been enough for you?" he asked.

"I would've preferred you in the flesh, but yes, this has been enough. If I had to choose between nothing and a ghost, you know I'd choose a ghost."

"But has me being here made things harder for you? Like with Tyler?" he asked.

"You're talking as if you had a choice in this. Listen, mister, you're the most magical thing that has ever happened to me. You've changed everything for me, in ways I don't think I can even see yet."

"I hoped you would say that."

"I would've always wondered what might've been. Now I know," I said.

"Now *we* know." He held his hand up, in a move for me to spin around. I spun.

After a few minutes, he asked, "What happens after I leave?"

Lisa was an example of what my life would look like if I couldn't let Finn go. I placed my hand over my heart. "I'll keep you here and keep on living."

I wanted to bottle this night and these feelings up, but there was no catching them. Just after midnight, shivering uncontrollably, I unplugged the bulb strands. I'd fought off the chill on my bare arms and shoulders for hours. Not wanting the romance of the night to end, I lit candles inside. I made hot chocolate, kicked off my shoes, and wrapped myself in a blanket on the couch. Finn sat close.

I reached for him. The energy flow between us was weaker than it had been outside.

"What's happening?" I asked.

He smiled sadly, "You're okay."

He'd said he'd stay until we were all okay. I closed my eyes, thinking about the hurt parts inside of me that I could now name. Before the truth about my past, I didn't know what had gone wrong. All my life, my turtle shell had kept me from breaking apart. But maybe it had held my brokenness hostage instead. The only way to heal was to be real with what I felt. Finn's love had made it possible.

I wasn't sure I knew what okay felt like, but maybe this was it.

"Does that mean we're almost out of time?" I wanted to grab onto him and make him stay. Even if I was okay. Even if we were all okay.

"We have enough time," he said.

"Enough time for what?"

"To get everyone to okay."

"But how long is that?" I asked.

"I don't think it will be long," he said. "There is one thing I'd like you to do for me."

"Anything," I said.

"You sure about that?" he asked.

"You wouldn't ask me to do something that wasn't good for me, so yes. Anything."

"I noticed you haven't opened your college letters."

Right. Those. I had pushed that decision away, not wanting to have to make it.

"They came the week you died and I kind of didn't care anymore. Then you were here. Then Lisa happened. I've always wanted to get away from her. Now I'm not sure that's the right thing anymore."

"Can you open them now, even if you aren't sure?"

Finn's loving nudge was a kindness that I would soon no longer have access to. "Yes," I said.

Finn's energy hovered sweetly beside me as I lined the letters upside down on the coffee table.

"They're thick. That means you got in, right?"

"That's what everyone says." I looked at him. "Finn?"

"What's up?"

"I'm sorry you won't be going to college."

"Thank you, but I don't want you to be sad for me. This is your moment. This is your life."

I wanted it to be about us, not just me.

"Claire, it's okay. Open them."

I lifted the flap of the first one. I'd only applied to schools in California, with the closest one being an hour away.

After reading four of the five acceptances my gut instincts remained quiet. When I got to the last one, the hairs on my arms stood up. "San Diego."

The school was close enough to see Lisa if I wanted to. The best part was I'd be close to my newfound family.

"San Diego," I said again.

"There you go! I'm proud of you, Goodnight," Finn said.

"It's happy dance time, isn't it?"

"You know it!" He stood up on the couch and started dancing.

I laughed.

"Get up here!" he said.

We danced.

He was right. I was mostly okay. It would hurt to no longer have him with me, but because of him, I knew I'd be okay without him.

Our dance moves were cut short by headlights piercing the half-darkness of the living room.

"Is that Lisa?" Finn asked.

"She said she'd find a place to stay."

A car door closed, and I heard female voices arguing.

"Let me find out," Finn said.

Another door slammed as Finn moved through the front door. The arguing got louder. Finn rushed back in just before the knock on the door.

"It's Vi and Kelly," Finn said.

"Huh? What are they doing here?"

"I'm pretty sure Vi is wasted."

"Vi? Oh, how am I going to explain this?" I clutched at my dress.

"I don't know, but my sister…"

I wrapped a blanket around my shoulders and pulled open the door.

Finn's sister stumbled forward, trying to move out from under the grasp of Kelly's arm. Violet's hair hung messy at her shoulders, she wore eye makeup and wasn't wearing her glasses. "I'm fine," she slurred.

"You aren't fine," Kelly said. Her blond hair loose over Finn's letterman jacket.

She's still wearing his jacket? Seriously?

"What are you doing here?" I asked.

Violet glared at Kelly. "See, she's not asleep!"

"So she's not. What's with the dress?" Kelly asked.

"You look bea-u-ti-ful," Violet said.

Ignoring Kelly, I turned to Finn's sister. "What's going on, Violet?" I asked again.

It was Kelly who answered me. "We were at the same party. She ran up and just started yelling at me."

"Yeah, because you're stu-pid," Violet said.

Kelly rolled her eyes. "When I realized she was drunk I told her I was taking her home. But she made me bring her here instead."

"I can't let my parents see me...like this. Can I stay here, Goodnight?" She giggled. "*Goodnight.* Cause Finn used to call her that," she told Kelly.

Kelly huffed.

"Of course, you can stay here," I assured Violet. "But I will have to call your dad."

"In the morning, okay?" Violet asked.

I nodded.

"Now that's settled, are you going to tell us why you're wearing that dress?" Kelly asked.

I wanted to reply with a snark like hers, but before I could Violet said, "No, no, no. Big fat nope. Instead, you tell us why you're wearing Finn's jacket. Now." She stamped her foot.

"Not this again." Kelly sighed.

Violet reached out and grabbed one of the sleeves. "It's not yours! Give it back!"

Kelly pulled her arm away. I jumped forward, dropping the blanket, and wrapped my arms around Violet, holding her back.

"You wear it like you won it. You're not a winner!" Violet said.

Kelly straightened her shoulders. "Knock it off, Violet. I wear it because I miss him."

"You miss him, huh? You think I don't? You think my mom and dad don't? It belongs to us," Violet spat at her.

Kelly sucked in her breath and wiped at her face.

"He didn't even want you anymore! He wanted Claire!" Violet began to cry.

Finn moved toward Violet but stopped himself before he got too close. I knew he'd wrap his arms around her if he could. He'd tried to make it all better, but he couldn't.

Kelly looked at me, then back to Violet. "He wasn't in his right mind," Kelly said.

"Bullshit. There were no signs of someone with a brain hemorrhage. His mind was perf-fect-ly fine!"

Kelly flung her hair back, saying nothing.

"He wasted all his time with you. Goodnight...she was the one."

Kelly shook her head, looking away.

"You know what? I don't care if you believe me or not. We know the truth." Violet touched my arm.

"Did you ever go out with him?" Kelly asked me.

"Yes," I said.

Finn sighed. "I've never seen her be this mean before. I'm sorry you have to deal with this."

Kelly smirked. "Yeah, right."

"Seriously?" I asked.

As if she'd proved a point, Kelly said, "Well, then!"

"If you could *see* him, the way that I can, you'd know it was me he was standing next to and me he wants to be with," I said.

For the second time, in a roundabout way, I had told someone that Finn was here, and it released some of the tightness in my chest.

"You're crazy," Kelly said.

"I truly don't care what you believe," I said.

"Boom!" Violet yelled.

"I know he'd be grateful that you brought Violet here and I am too. Thank you for that, sincerely. However, I'm also sure he'd be extremely disappointed that you're keeping his jacket from his family and talking to us like this."

She pulled the jacket tighter around her. "You can't know that, either."

"What do you honestly think Finn would think of you right now?" I asked.

Kelly dropped her arms to her sides.

Finn moved beside Kelly and whispered in her ear, "Give it back."

She looked from me to Violet, took a few steps back on the porch, and then slowly removed Finn's jacket. Violet stepped toward her and held her arms out. Kelly slowly handed it to her.

Violet hugged it. "Finn," she said.

Kelly shuddered as Finn whispered in her ear, "Thank you."

Without another word Kelly spun around, her hair flying behind her, and walked to her car.

Had she not been so Kelly-like, I might've felt sad for her. She probably really loved Finn, but I couldn't bring myself to feel sympathy for her.

Violet watched her drive away. "Good riddance. Thank you, Claire."

"I'm happy to have helped. Finn would want you to have his jacket." I held out my hand to her. "Now let's get your drunk butt inside and talk."

I got water for Violet, and we sat down at the kitchen table. Violet took a sip, then pushed the container away, making a face. She folded her arms on the table and rested her head on them.

"Have you thrown up yet?" I asked.

"On the way here... inside her car!" She laughed.

"This isn't your first time drinking, is it?"

Violet blinked and shook her head.

"I didn't picture you as a partier."

"Just since Finn..."

Finn winced, responsibility for his family's sorrow weighing on his already weak energy. I didn't know what Finn's "okay" barometer ratings were, but Violet's level couldn't be very high.

"It's not going to help, you know."

"Sometimes I just need to forget," she said.

"And do you?"

Violet shook her head and sighed. "Not for long." She put her head back down and mumbled, "No lecture, please. It's like I can hear Finn yelling at me now."

I looked over at Finn. "Good," Finn and I said simultaneously.

Once I had Violet tucked into the spare bedroom she asked. "Will you tell *me* why you're all dressed up?"

"Um, practice run?"

"For the prom?" Violet asked.

"Something like that," I said.

Violet closed her eyes and mumbled, "You would've gone with Finn."

Finn leaned over and kissed her head. "She did, little sister. Now go to sleep, and never drink again, at least not until you're twenty-one!"

"Uh-huh," she said before rolling over.

"It was hot to see you stand up to Kelly like that," Finn said when we were in my room.

I felt powerful and sexy with him looking at me the way he was.

We held our lips together, and even though his electric spark had been fading, I could still feel the electricity on my mouth.

"Come here," I said.

I backed toward the bathroom, drawing him to follow with a come-hither finger. I kept the door open until he entered the room behind me, slow and smiling. Not taking my eyes off his, I closed and locked the door.

I slipped the dress off my shoulders and shimmied out of it. Finn groaned as I leaned over and turned the shower on.

His desire was hot against my back, his energy tracing along my skin.

"Claire."

I removed my bra. "How about a shower?"

From the look in his eyes, he was being pulled forward by the promise of me.

I longed to be able to give myself to him fully. To feel myself a part of him. The water touched me in all the places I longed for him to caress.

Closing my eyes, I slid my fingers down and against myself. He moved, shifting his presence in and out of me until my face scrunched up and my lower half exploded with muscle spasms.

Our eyes met, fulfilled, as much as we possibly could be.

CHAPTER 22

The next morning, Finn watched me stretch my arms above my head and yawn. I wondered if he cataloged every look, conversation, and electrical touch we shared and tucked it away in his soul like I did.

"You never get bored just watching me?" I asked.

"Nope," he said. "I could watch you forever."

"Just in case you didn't know, I'm going to miss you, so much."

"I know, Goodnight. You know what else I know?" he asked.

"What?"

"You're so goddamn hot. The shower last night was…"

"Extremely hot," I said. A quick blush flushed my cheeks.

"How about an instant replay?" he asked.

"Do we have time?"

"For this, yes. But be quiet because I heard Lisa come home a few minutes ago."

He moved his energy against me. When I neared release, Finn put his fingers over my lips with a satisfied smile on his face. Silently I let go, feeling my heart beating between my legs.

Breathing hard, I rolled onto my side and pulled the blankets up to my chest. "You rock my world," I told him.

"You're amazing at rocking your own world," Finn said.

I blushed again but smiled. "I'll never forget this. Of course, not just this—all of it."

"Not being able to touch you has made this so hard," he said.

"That's what she said." I laughed.

Finn moved close to me, resting his head beside mine. "I didn't know it was possible to love another person this much."

I didn't know it was possible to be loved that much. "Me, either."

"Forever," he said.

"Forever," I said.

After a few minutes, I slipped my pajamas back on and asked, "Should we check on Vi?"

We peered into the spare room and listened to Violet snoring softly, an arm covering her eyes.

"I love that kid, but I hope she wakes up with the worst headache she's ever had." Finn said. "You should probably give Lisa a heads-up about Vi."

I nodded. "I'm going to shower now, in case there isn't time later before my shift," I said.

I grabbed a pair of jeans, a black knitted sweatshirt, and some black boots from my room then realized I'd picked out almost the same thing I'd worn on my first date with Finn.

"Good idea. You need to smell nice for your date with Tyler tonight," Finn said.

I flung my jeans at him. "Too soon. And it's not a date!"

Finn smiled and waved me away. "Take a shower, Goodnight. I'm going to hang with Vi."

In the kitchen, Lisa was stirring eggs. Her hair was down, and her face shone with youth and health. It made sense why people could mistake us for sisters.

"You look nice this morning," Lisa said. "Not that you don't always look nice. You're just looking freshly put together."

"I was thinking the same about you. I had a good night. I have work in a few hours and dinner with a friend later."

"How did the dress work out?"

"It was perfect," I said. My instinct to mumble, avoid eye contact, and retreat was gone. Like a butterfly opening its wings, my chest had expanded, and it had become easier to breathe around her.

"So, you had a good night?" she asked.

Goosebumps burst from my skin. "Best night of my life. Hands down. For real." I grabbed a coffee mug from the cabinet.

"That's awesome," she said.

A stack of papers on the counter made me pause. If she had more secrets to share, I would scream. "What's all that?" I asked.

"This will sound insane, which might not surprise you, but it's Mimi's will. It's my first time looking at it."

"Oh? You didn't need to sign anything?"

"I signed things. I just didn't pay attention to what I signed. I asked the lawyer to handle anything actionable, then I stuck it in my dresser drawer. Monthly checks started coming shortly after she died. She took such good care of us even after she was gone."

"I didn't realize she'd been helping financially."

"Thankfully so," Lisa said. "It filled in when I fell short. Unfortunately, it also allowed me to spend money on alcohol. An unintended consequence, I'm sure." She looked down. "The timing is pretty perfect since I saw the acceptance letters you left out."

"Oh. I got distracted and forgot to put them away," I said.

"I'm glad I saw them. Your grades must be stellar." She tilted her head and smiled.

"I've worked very hard."

"Then this will be good news. For once," she said. "Mimi left you money for college. For both of us, actually."

The floor shifted beneath me. When I looked up, Finn was in the kitchen smiling. He raised his hands in the air, kicked up his knees, and spun around in circles, doing his happy dance.

"It's probably not enough to cover everything, but it'll take care of a lot."

"Wow. I've been saving up, too, so…"

Just like that, Mimi had given me what I'd been striving for—a clean break from Lisa.

"If you want to go to one of the more expensive schools further away and need more money, I'll do what I can to help. I'd love for you to be close, but I have no right to ask you to stay."

"Actually, I've decided on San Diego. Not too far, but close to Grammy Sarah and the rest of the family." Family wasn't a word that I said often, and it sounded strange coming out of my mouth.

Lisa half-smiled and mumbled, "Oh, yes, that makes sense."

"It's close enough for weekend visits. And maybe breaks, too."

"It is," she said.

"You never finished school?" I asked.

"I'd planned to go back after I had you and Sophia, but obviously that never happened. I'm considering becoming a grief therapist." Her eyes lit up.

"Cool," I said.

"I've been inspired by the people who are helping me."

"I think that's great. I've considered therapy too or maybe English…"

Finn rushed in. "Violet's coming down," he said.

"Any chance you have enough eggs for three?" I asked.

"Three?" Lisa asked.

Violet walked slowly into the room, her eyes on the floor. Finn stood beside her.

"Hello," Lisa said to Violet. Then asked me, "Was this who came over last night?"

"Um, yes and no. It wasn't a planned visit. This is Finn's sister."

"Violet?" Lisa asked.

Violet raised her head to look at Lisa, confused.

"Hi, I'm Lisa. I know your dad a little. He mentioned you and Finn." She cleared her throat, then turned to grab three plates from the cupboard.

"How do you know my dad?" Violet asked.

I pulled a water bottle from the fridge and handed it to her.

Her question went unanswered, but she let it go, taking a long sip of the water. I dropped two Advil into her hand. She swallowed them then sank onto a stool, her head in both hands.

After a minute, she abruptly stood and ran toward the downstairs bathroom, and we heard her vomit.

"Hangover?" Lisa asked.

I nodded.

"We should call Eric," Lisa said.

"I told her I would," I said.

"She's too young to be drinking."

"Yeah, but some people use it as a coping mechanism, right?"

"Okay, I deserved that, but this isn't about me," Lisa said. She handed me the wooden spoon. "I'm sure she won't be hungry, but she can have mine if she is. Can you dish them out? I'll go check on her."

I turned to Finn who had returned to my side and said, "Hey, do you remember when I said I might need your help with my family at some point?"

"Of course," I said.

"It's time."

My stomach dropped. It was as if we were nearing the climax of a movie and we had no control over what would happen or when it would end.

Mimi had been all over Finn and his time here. Did she have control of our timeline? Could I ask for more? Beg?

I squeezed my eyes shut, hoping to deflect the inevitable. "If it's time for me to help, does it mean it's almost time for you to go?" I asked.

He frowned, "I'm not leaving, yet. But I do need to call in that favor now."

Eric arrived ten minutes after Lisa called him. Violet's body shook with sobs when he came in.

He rushed to where she was sitting on the couch and put his arms around her. "Oh, Violet. It's okay, everything will be okay."

The gap of missing out on a dad of my own splintered through me like a lightning bolt.

Lisa and I went to the kitchen to give them space. We picked at the eggs on our plates and took long sips of coffee.

"We need to help the Petersons," I said.

"Help them how?" Lisa asked.

"By sharing our story."

Until I'd said it, I'd had no idea what I could do to help them—how I could ease Mrs. Peterson's grief or make her want to live again when her firstborn couldn't.

She nodded, "Eric's story woke me up. Maybe the timing was just right," she said.

I rolled my eyes. Eighteen years was far beyond what should be considered the right timing.

"That must sound terrible to you. Mimi took care of you, so, it was easy to stay stuck."

I clenched my fists. "You didn't try. Don't blame Mimi for your mistakes."

"I'm not blaming her, Claire."

"You're responsible for your own life and the choices you made. I heard Mimi beg you to get help many times," I said.

"It hurt too much to look at my pain. We can only begin to heal when we're ready," she said.

"No matter if talking to the Petersons together works or not, it's important to me that I do everything in my power to help Finn's family."

As I said it aloud, I knew what being successful would mean. Finn moving on, sooner rather than later. Even if it meant losing him faster, it was the right thing to do.

Finn, Eric, and Violet entered the kitchen.

"Thanks for calling me, I think we'll head out now." Eric said.

"I'd like to talk to Mrs. Peterson, the three of you, really. Is it okay if Lisa and I follow you home?"

Eric looked from me to Lisa, "Really?" Eric asked.

"Claire thinks sharing what we've gone through might help. Like you helped me," Lisa said.

"How did you help her, Dad?" Violet asked.

A hint of betrayal lurked in the air. All eyes were on Eric. According to Lisa nothing had happened between her and Eric, but he had been in her bedroom and that would be difficult to explain away.

"Um, well, I've been going to a grief group. After the meetings, some of us go to a bar nearby. I met Lisa there."

"You go to the grief group, too?" Violet asked Lisa.

"No. We met at the bar. My intent had always been to go to the group. I tried once a week for over a year to go inside, but I couldn't do it. I always ended up drinking instead."

She hadn't told me she'd thought about getting help. This revelation made my heart expand for her even more, making room for hope.

The domino effect of Finn dying brought our parents together, which led to Lisa's rehab, and the revelation and truth of my beginnings. An unfortunate reason for the sliding door moment that altered the course of my life—or rather all our lives—but necessary all the same.

"Did you...sleep with her?" Violet asked.

Eric dropped his head down. "No, but..."

"Nothing happened," Lisa said.

"God, Dad! Everything is such a mess!" Violet spun to him, her hand flung through Finn, but she didn't notice.

Finn's color had faded since his dad and Violet walked into the room. His energy was likely fading, too.

"I know, honey." Eric put his hand on Violet's shoulder, but she pulled away.

"Goodnight, can you get us over to my mom?" Finn asked.

I stood up, looking at my watch. The pressure of time running out seared into my heart. "Sorry to interrupt, but I have to be at work in a few hours," I said.

"So, we're doing this now?" Eric asked.

"Yes," Finn and I said in unison.

"It has to be now," Finn said.

I steadied myself by leaning against the kitchen counter. Finn quickly moved to me, his electric touch less vibrant, but it was enough to center me.

"I'm still here," he said.

I leaned into him and reminded myself to breathe. "We're all here now. It just makes sense," I said.

We headed out together, apprehensive but hopeful.

CHAPTER 23

"Honk your horn. One long and two quick," Finn said.

I pulled up in front of his house and followed his instructions without question.

"What are you doing?" Lisa asked.

"Trusting my gut," I said.

Finn's mom rushed out of the front door. She stood on the porch and scanned the yard.

The grass was unkempt, long, and full of weeds. Several purple flowers planted up against the house sagged, thirsty and weak.

Like a team hitting the court for a big game, we walked across the grass to Molly.

Her eyes narrowed. "That was Finn's honk. Who did that?"

"Tell her my dad did it," Finn said.

"Wasn't it you, Mr. Peterson?" I winked at him.

He raised his eyebrows at me, then quickly complied. "I just wanted to get your attention, Molly."

"That was cruel," she said.

Eric stepped back as if he'd been slapped.

Violet walked forward, clutching Finn's letterman jacket like a child holding a blanket. "Mom, this is Claire and her mom, Lisa," she said.

"Why are they here?" she asked.

"Come on, Mom," Finn said, and then assured me, "She's usually friendly."

"Mom, you remember Claire. She's the girl Finn called Goodnight," Violet said.

Molly turned to me. "Oh, it is you!"

"Hello again, Mrs. Peterson. Your spaghetti was delicious," I said.

"Ah, yes, I'd forgotten about that. Thank you."

Finn's anxious energy bounced between us, and I wasn't sure how to begin the intervention with his mom. Selfishly, I thought the fact that she, like Violet, was far from okay might give me more time with Finn. Though I would never wish for them to keep suffering.

Lisa stepped forward. "I know words are meaningless at a time like this, but I'm sorry for your loss."

Molly nodded. "I appreciate that, but why are you all here?"

"Eric told me what happened to your family, and it changed my life. Claire and I wanted to talk to you about our family," Lisa said.

She glared at Eric, then looked back to Lisa, "Why would Eric tell you about me?"

"Molly, nothing happened, but I spent a night with her. Just talking. It was an interesting coincidence that Lisa turned out to be Goodnight—or rather, Claire's—mom."

Violet shuffled her feet. Molly stared at Eric, her eyes fixed.

"Aren't you going to say something?" Eric's voice cracked.

"What do you want me to say?" she asked.

"Something. Anything, really! You've got to wake up, Molly. You aren't the only one who's missing Finn."

Her eyes flashed at him. "You weren't the one who found him that morning," she said.

"You didn't either. I found him." Violet's voice was barely audible.

I turned to Violet and said, "Say it again."

Violet cleared her throat. "I went in to wake him up that morning. I was the first one to touch him, to realize that he was...gone. Why do you think Dad came back? I called him. It was me who found him!" The threat of sobs deepened her voice.

Molly looked down at her from the raised porch. "I don't remember you being in there."

"You would've known if you'd ever talked to me." Her shoulders rose, as if the weight of her pain had begun to lift.

"I...I don't know what to say..." Molly said.

"We're all at a loss," Eric said.

"You don't seem to be lonely though." Molly waved a hand toward Lisa.

"You haven't been talking to me, either! Though I hadn't seen her again until today. Claire called me to pick up Violet from their house. Anyway, please just listen. I think they can help us with Finn."

"I'll never get over Finn!" Molly said.

"Of course you won't," Lisa said.

"That's not what I meant," Eric said. "They have a similar story to ours."

"I don't want any help." Molly turned to go back inside.

"Goodnight, please get my mom back." Finn touched me. I could barely feel it.

"Wait!" I called out. "Finn is... *was* very important to me. I'm here for him."

Molly slowly turned around, wriggling her hands together.

I walked up the three steps to her. My peripheral vision disappeared. Every ounce of love that Finn had given me pushed me toward her.

Molly was a few inches taller than me, so I looked up at her. "First, I want to thank you for Finn."

"Oh." Her lips trembled and her tired eyes turned glossy with tears.

"I've loved him for a long time. I only want to help, for his sake."

"You're a sweetheart, aren't you?" She reached for my hand.

I squeezed hers. "Can we sit?"

We continued to hold hands and shuffled to the rustic yellow bench on their porch. Finn floated up to sit beside me. Lisa, Eric, and Violet gathered on the steps.

I closed my eyes, searching my heart for the right words to bring her to okay.

Opening them, I said, "I can't compare my grief to yours, but I've lost people, too." I took a deep breath. "The role I play in this story is that of a daughter, like Violet. It's the parallels between us that matter."

I turned to Finn. "Is this okay?" I intended the question for him, but Molly squeezed my hand and responded.

"Yes, please go on."

Finn smiled and nodded at me. His touch on my shoulder sent only tiny shocks of electricity through me.

"I recently found out that my dad and twin sister died on the day I was born."

Molly put her hand to her mouth.

"And the reason I didn't know till now is because their deaths were kept from me. Lisa is my mother, but she didn't raise me. My Mimi—her mom—did. And ever since she died, I've been taking care of myself. Honestly, Lisa was like a stranger to me, and I never felt loved by her."

I didn't turn to see how what I was saying affected Lisa. It didn't matter—it was my truth.

"Once I learned about everything she'd gone through, the way she acted toward me made more sense, but it didn't make it better. She ignored me because I reminded her of what she'd lost. It took hearing pain like hers to finally get her to rehab."

"That's terrible," she said.

"I can't begin to imagine what it feels like to lose a child. I know it hasn't been that long since Finn passed, but time goes quicker than we think. Lisa lost eighteen years of her life and I lost a mother. I want to offer a view of what could happen if you don't get help. Mr. Peterson and Violet feel like they have not only lost Finn, but you too. I don't think you all have to lose each other like I lost everyone. I know Finn wouldn't want that for you."

Molly looked over at Violet and her husband. Eric clutched Violet's hand and they nodded their confirmation of what I'd said. Lisa's head was pressed back against the house and her eyes were closed.

"Finn would want an alternative ending for you and Violet," I said.

I beckoned Violet closer. "Violet, can you tell your mom how you ended up at my house last night?"

Eric released her hand and helped her up. I motioned for Violet to take my place on the bench. Violet sat down, still holding Finn's jacket.

Molly reached for it and asked, "Where did you get this?"

"I got it back from Kelly. She's the one who took me to Claire's. Kelly was at the same party. I was drunk and went after her."

"Drunk? No, Vi..."

"I know, but...it's been so hard. I've been so alone."

Eric came over and knelt beside his daughter.

"Did you know?" Molly asked Eric.

"Only since this morning."

"Oh, Vi. I'm so sorry I didn't see it," she said.

"It's not your fault," Violet said. Tears fell from her eyes. "But like Goodnight said, Dad and I are still here. We need you and you need us."

Her parents leaned forward and put their arms around her.

Finn stood close, but just out of reach from them and me, making space for letting go.

"We should've noticed," Eric said. "We've been caught up in our own pain."

Molly looked over at Lisa who sat with her hands clasped in her lap. The two mothers nodded at each other and then Lisa walked away toward my car.

"I'm sorry," Molly said to no one in particular. "Finn not being here is unbearable. Some days I don't know how I can keep going."

"I feel that way too," Eric said. "I miss Finn every single second. I miss everything about our life. Can we get help to work through this together?"

"Yes," Violet said.

Molly nodded.

Finn bounced in place beside his mending family.

They were going to be okay. Not right away, but they were on the path to it.

And eventually, Lisa and I were going to be okay, too.

My body began to ache, not knowing what to do with the dread of Finn almost leaving.

Finn looked over at me. "You did it. Exactly as I knew you would because you're the most amazing girlfriend in the entire world. Look at them!"

I nodded, unable to reply without being overheard, a bittersweet smile on my face.

"I'm not leaving yet. We'll get our goodbye," he said.

I turned to go, knowing Finn would want to have some sort of goodbye with his family.

"Wait," Molly said. She stood up and embraced me. "I can see what my boy saw in you. Thank you for loving him and looking out for us."

Eric and Violet wrapped their arms around both of us. After a minute, we unraveled from each other. Finn wrapped his energy around all of us and winked at me.

"I owe a lot to Finn, and this was all for him. I know you'll be okay," I squeezed her hand and nodded at Mr. Peterson. "I should get back to Lisa. I'll see you at school, Vi."

"Goodnight, thank you for everything," Violet said.

Lisa looked up as I approached her. "I can't take any credit for how amazing you are. You'll be a rock-star therapist if that's what you decide to do. I'm so sorry I didn't see you all those years. I hope someday you'll be able to forgive me and will one day see me as your mom."

"I get a little bit closer every day." I would go to therapy with her. I would work on trusting her, on letting her be a mom to me. I'd do it for Mimi. But mostly for the little girl inside me and the woman I'd become, who had always been worthy of a mom's love.

"I know it'll be hard to make up for lost time," she said.

"It'll be impossible," I told her.

"I'm going to try."

"Let's just start from here."

"Deal," she said. "Someday, if it's not too much to ask, I'd like you to call me Mom again."

"You never responded when I did. So, I stopped," I said.

"I know."

"That might take some time."

"Take all the time you need. Ready to go home?" she asked.

"Yeah, I have to get to work soon."

"Goodnight, wait!" Violet ran toward us, Finn's letterman jacket still in her arms. "You've changed everything."

"It wasn't just me." I looked at Finn, still standing with his parents.

Violet held Finn's jacket out to me. "We want you to have this."

"Really?"

She smiled. "Yes. Finn chose you and I know you would've ended up with it eventually. We can get it dry cleaned first if you want to get the smell of Kelly off."

I laughed and took the jacket from her outstretched hands. "Are you sure about this?" I asked.

"Here, let me help you put it on."

The heavy jacket sank onto my shoulders, wrapping Finn's presence around me. He beamed at me from the porch and nodded approvingly. I knew I wouldn't keep his jacket, just as I couldn't keep him. His jacket belonged with his family and Finn belonged to the universe. Yet, for a small pocket of time, they'd both been mine.

CHAPTER 24

The pull of Finn going sent shivers of panic through me. Work was the last place I wanted to be, but I went begrudgingly at his request. Co-workers moved around me, human blurs in black shirts. Amid the familiar sounds of ringing phones and drivers talking, I sauced, cheesed, and topped pizzas on autopilot.

Standing in a corner of the room, Finn watched me work, one leg bent, his socked foot pressed against the wall. Only a light gleam of energy now, but still clear enough to see.

My handsome-as-hell ghost boyfriend smiled at me. I wanted to keep him, but it wouldn't be fair to stop him from his "okay." Even a big, bold wish at our dandelion meadow wouldn't stop what we'd always known.

This time, his leaving would be forever.

My only control was in acceptance. But it hurt.

An hour before my dinner with Tyler, Finn found me in the freezer reorganizing the cheese boxes. My breath created pale white puffs in the cold air, like the consistency of Finn's form.

"I'll see you after, okay?"

I pushed the last box of cheese in place. "After? Maybe I should just cancel so we can spend more time together."

"Remember, you asked him to dinner. To fix things between you." His tone left me no room to push back; he'd made up his mind. And he was right.

"Can you promise I'll see you again?"

He held up a pinky finger. "I swear…not on my life, of course, but on my love."

I nodded and watched him disappear.

The moment of truth with Tyler had finally arrived. I contemplated how I'd explain what happened in the manager's office that day. Lost in thought, I didn't notice Tyler come in until I turned to put a pizza in the oven. There he was.

"Hey," he said.

He was clean shaven, his short blond hair spiked up, his cologne scent heavier than I was used to. It was rare for me to see him in anything other than his uniform, but now he wore jeans and a black hoodie—seeing him in the same outfit Finn had been stuck in for months, was not lost on me.

"Hi," I said, surprised by the blush that spread over my face and the sudden rush of butterflies. Reacting this way to Tyler confused me.

"I'm early, but I just wanted to let you know I'm here. I'll wait outside."

At six, I clocked out. In the bathroom, I scrubbed my hands with soap several times to remove the pizza smell. I changed into my jeans and sweater, ran a brush through my hair, and reapplied some makeup. Pausing to look at my reflection, I realized this was the first time I'd prepared myself physically for dinner with Tyler. An unfamiliar stirring buzzed inside me. Sighing, I tossed my lip gloss back into my purse without putting it on.

Outside, Tyler waited for me, his head down, his thumb scrolling on the phone in his hand. My stomach flipped when he looked up.

"You look nice," he said.

"So do you," I said.

My own phone rang, and I jumped with surprise. Julia's name and face appeared on the screen. I held it up to show him who was calling.

"Cool, let's talk to her," he said.

I pressed accept and positioned myself, so Tyler and I were both visible on the screen.

"Aw, hi, guys! The three musketeers are back together again."

We laughed.

"Actually, can we make it four?" Julia asked. She repositioned herself, and a girl with curly brown hair and deep blue eye shadow smiled at us.

"Wait, a minute—are we finally meeting Tanya?" I asked.

Tanya laughed. "In the flesh—well, sort of."

Her joke reminded me of Finn. I looked around for him, but he wasn't there. So many things would remind me of him after he was gone.

"I've heard so much about you two," Tanya said.

"We're pretty awesome, but we heard you are, too," Tyler said.

Julia's face was shiny with happiness.

We talked for a few minutes before Julia acknowledged that she knew we had a dinner to get to. She winked at me before hanging up.

Julia wasn't on Finn's list of people who needed to be okay, but she was on mine. And she was okay now, too.

Remnants of sunlight hung visible on the horizon. The light posts clicked on simultaneously as we walked across the parking lot.

Tyler asked for a corner table, away from the heavily bussed area. Out of our element, we sat across from each other, timid smiles on our faces. We ordered and made small talk until the food came. I'd only snacked for lunch and hungrily dug into my enchiladas.

After we'd eaten about half our meals, Tyler put his fork down. I raised my eyes to his.

"Can we talk about that day in the office?" he asked.

"Yes," I said, knowing I should've been the one to start this conversation. Still undecided on what I needed to say, I'd been delaying.

"I remember you crying and us hugging before I blacked out. When I came to, we were kissing, and then you pushed me away. Not that I wouldn't want to kiss you, but I don't think I did. So that means you must've kissed me. Yet that doesn't really feel right, either. Especially because you pushed me away."

Stalling, I picked up my glass of iced tea and sipped through the straw, hoping to suck up a response.

"After you left, I got such a bad headache. Maybe the office was gassed or something? I'm struggling here. Do you know what happened, Claire?"

There were only two options—the truth or a lie. I could lose him no matter what, and that made my stomach churn. The truth carried with it the possibility that Tyler would think I was crazy. A lie would further divide us and eat away at me. I wanted him in my life, and I realized I never wanted to lie to him again.

"I know what happened, and it's not what you're probably thinking."

"I didn't force myself on you, did I? God, I couldn't forgive myself if I did." He rubbed his forehead.

"No, Tyler, it wasn't like that," I said.

"I have to know what happened. No matter what it is, Claire, you have to tell me!"

"You'll think I'm crazy."

"I feel like *I'm* going crazy."

"It was Finn," I said, like I had that day at work, only this time I would tell him everything.

"Huh? What was Finn?" he asked.

I took a deep breath. "It was Finn's ghost in your body who kissed me."

"*What?*"

"I can see his ghost," I said.

Tyler's jaw dropped.

The waitress approached the table and refilled our drinks. I poked at my food with my fork while she poured and murmured a thank you before she walked away.

"Say something," I said.

"Finn is a ghost, and he was inside my body?"

I nodded.

"And he kissed you, using my lips?" He touched his lips with the tips of two fingers.

"It wasn't planned or even something Finn thought he could do, but..."

"You knew about this and didn't tell me, after all this time?"

"I tried to talk to you. You didn't reply to my texts. You changed your schedule at work. You didn't make it easy to tell you."

"I was hurt because I thought…Shit, what the hell, Claire?"

"I'm sorry, Tyler." I searched his eyes, looking for a way to make us better.

"It's a violation of…my body, my privacy, my free will."

"I know. It sounds horrible. It is horrible. I wish I could take it all back. Finn felt terrible. We both did."

Tyler looked around. "Is he here now?"

"He's still here on Earth, but he's not here with us. He'll actually be leaving very soon, I think." My voice caught, but I held back my tears. This moment wasn't about me; it was about Tyler.

"This is unreal. How is this even possible?" he asked.

"We think he stayed behind because we had unfinished business."

"Was part of the unfinished business to kiss you?"

"No. Like I said, that wasn't planned. The unfinished business was much deeper than that."

Tyler pushed his plate away. My appetite was gone, too.

He listened while I explained the way Finn's death and his family had ultimately led Lisa to rehab. "He's the reason why I'm sitting here now," I said.

"What do you mean?"

"He knows you care about me. He wants to make sure we're…"

"Wait—you wouldn't be here with me if it wasn't for him?" He pushed his chair back, the wood scraping the floor.

"That's not what I meant. I wanted to explain it and for us to be okay again."

Tyler stood up. I reached out for him, but he stepped back. He called out to the waitress, "Can we get the bill over here, please?"

"Tyler, please don't go."

"I need to process this."

"I've got the bill," I said.

"I'll meet you outside." He rushed out the door.

I sighed with relief that he didn't tell me to leave. Maybe he didn't plan on exiting my life again.

I paid the bill when it came, brushing off the waitress's questions, but didn't get up to leave—from my seat by the window, I could see Tyler pacing back and forth. Squeezing my hands in my lap, I waited for a sign of an appropriate time to join him.

My turtle shell threatened to swallow me up, but I fought the urge to sneak away. I owed it to the three of us to face the truth. Finn had lost his chance to live. The least I could do was jump into my life with both feet, knowing that everything would be okay, even if I fell.

At times Tyler walked slowly with his hands on his head. Other times, he ran circles around the parking lot, his arms pumping at his sides.

I imagined the thoughts going through his head. If I hadn't been able to see Finn with my own eyes, I wouldn't have believed he was there, either. Asking Tyler to believe me was a big deal.

After about twenty minutes, Tyler finally stopped in the middle of the parking lot. That was my sign to go outside.

I expected to see Finn waiting for me too, but he wasn't there. He couldn't be gone, not yet. He'd promised.

Stepping quietly, I made my way to Tyler. My hair fell into my face, and I pushed it away, fully exposed. His back was to me. When he heard me approach, he turned to face me. My heartbeat quickened.

"I believe you," he said.

My breath came out in a *whoosh*—one I felt like I'd been holding since that day in the office. If Finn were here, he would've been doing his happy dance.

"You wouldn't tell me this if it wasn't true," he said.

"I wouldn't," I said.

"Does Julia know?" he asked.

"You're the only one I've told."

"Finally, I get to know something before Julia," he smiled, slightly.

"Yes, you do," I said.

One day, I would tell Julia everything.

"I guess it does explain some things. When did you start seeing him?"

"The day of his memorial."

"Makes sense. Your mood changed then."

I nodded. "I went from being heartbroken to happy in a second."

"You're in love with him."

"I am," I said.

"And of course, he's absolutely in love with you, too, because why wouldn't he be? I can't really blame him. I'm sure I would've jumped into a random body, too, if it meant being with you."

His eyes met mine, sure and honest. I didn't want to look away, and I didn't.

"What other business remains unfinished between you two?" he asked.

"The only thing that's left for him, I think, is between me and you."

"Me and you?" he asked.

"I'm not sure what he's hoping for, but yes, it has to do with us."

He took a step toward me, and then suddenly Finn was there, next to Tyler. I looked from one to the other, my heart split between them.

Tyler looked at the empty space beside him. "He's here?"

"Yes, right beside you," I said.

Finn put his hand on Tyler's shoulder.

Tyler shuddered and stepped away. "What was that?"

"He touched you," I said.

"Does he want something?" Tyler asked.

I looked at Finn.

"Clearly, you told him the truth," Finn said.

"That's what you wanted, isn't it?" I asked.

"It doesn't matter what I wanted. I agree with your decision, though."

"Good," I said.

"Can you tell him I'm sorry?" Finn asked.

I relayed the message and Tyler said, "Apology weirdly accepted."

"And tell him to take good care of you. I know you don't need him, but if you end up together...you only deserve the best."

I wasn't going to tell Tyler that.

"Loving someone else doesn't mean you loved me any less," Finn said.

This was it. The beginning of our goodbye.

"What's he saying?" Tyler asked.

"It's time for me to go," Finn said.

Tears slid down my cheeks, "He's leaving," I said.

Tyler stepped forward. "Okay, man, you can borrow my body again—but just for a kiss."

Finn and I stared at Tyler in disbelief.

"But first, I need to ask you something, Claire. I know this is awkward timing, considering you're in love with a ghost, but I still have to ask. Do we have a chance? Do I have a chance with you?"

Tyler had just done what Finn and I hadn't until it was almost too late. He'd put his heart out there, even if it meant being rejected. I looked at the two great guys in front of me.

Finn said, "Just because you were the love of my life doesn't mean I'm yours. Don't worry about my feelings, Goodnight. Let your heart respond."

If they'd both been living, breathing men asking me to love them, I wouldn't know how to choose. But I didn't have to. Finn was never meant to stay.

Tyler stood before me with his heart in his hand, so full of trust in me, and willing to let me say goodbye to Finn in his body. I hadn't been brave enough to know what my heart wanted or deserved, but now I knew.

My love for Finn ran deep—an old, familiar, soulmate kind of love. With Tyler, it was new and undiscovered, a safe place to be me, and just as true.

"Yes, there is a chance. But I have to tell you, I'm going to college in San Diego next year, so I don't know what that might mean for us…"

He raised his eyebrows. "San Diego? I've been considering transferring there; I have enough units. Besides, it's not that far away, even if I don't."

"What about Palm Row Pizza?" I asked.

"I'm not going to run my uncle's business forever—I want to start a business of my own. But you said *yes*. Everything else is cake from here." He smiled.

"Okay," I smiled.

Tyler held his arms up. "I'm ready."

"He's definitely a good guy—I knew it all along," Finn smiled. "Thank him for his generous offer, but you can tell him we're good."

"But..." I said.

"Trust me," Finn said.

I turned to Tyler and relayed the message.

"Is he leaving?" Tyler asked.

Finn nodded, so I did, too.

Tyler squeezed my hand reassuringly, "Claire, I'm going to go, so you can say goodbye. We'll talk later or tomorrow or whenever you're ready," he looked to the air next to me and said, "Good luck on your journey, man."

Finn touched our hands, spreading electricity up my fingers and arm. Tyler's expression confirmed he felt it, too.

We watched Tyler walk away. Before he turned the corner, he raised his hand to wave, then was out of sight.

This side of the mall closed early, and the parking lot was already empty. To an onlooker, I stood alone beneath the light pole, as if a spotlight was directed at me.

Finn and I stood face to face.

"She's here," he said, glancing over my shoulder.

"Mimi?" I asked.

He nodded. "The light around her is beautiful, Goodnight. Like it was before."

I couldn't see what he was seeing.

"Can I talk to her?" I asked.

"She can't speak in a way that you will hear her, but she's right beside you."

My body temperature increased as if a warm cocoon of love had wrapped itself around me. I'd been so mad at her for leaving me, for keeping such big secrets, but it was time to let that go.

Deep down, I knew she'd never meant to hurt me, that everything she'd kept from me had been to protect me, even if I didn't agree with it. Loving someone didn't make you immune from hurting them—and I had always known she loved me.

Something brushed across my forehead, and it felt the way her goodnight kisses used to feel—quick, but firm and true. The air around me cooled—but she didn't feel gone.

"Did she leave?" I asked.

"She's still here. She said she has something for you, and it's going to take a lot of energy."

"What is it?"

"It all makes sense now," he said. "She did keep me here for you. Lisa meeting my dad wasn't a coincidence—everything has been guided. She wasn't sure it would work, and she knew she was breaking some rules of the universe, but she said you were worth it. She wanted you to know the truth and she wanted your wish for me to come true."

The magic of everything had been because of Mimi. She'd given me a second chance with Finn, connected our families, and sent me the dream that led me to the boxes filled with answers to questions I hadn't known I needed to ask. Through all that, Lisa had received what she needed to begin healing. While Finn's family would struggle through grief, at least they would do it together.

Suddenly, the sound of shattering glass echoed through the lot. It took me several seconds to realize that one by one, each bulb in the parking lot was exploding—until only one remained burning—the one I stood beneath. Shards rained down slowly like silver glitter in the air.

Later, I would find tiny pieces of it in my hair—proof that this had all been *real*.

Just as I had begun to process what had happened, Finn stepped toward me a solid, physical being. Still with his perpetual bedhead and socked feet.

My breath caught in my throat as I grabbed at his sweatshirt, wanting to hold on to his existence. He put his hands on my cheeks.

I searched his bright green eyes, questioning my sanity but trusting that Mimi had found a way to give me one last gift—a physical goodbye with Finn.

"How did she do it?" I asked.

"Magic?" he shrugged, smiling. "She's not sure how long we have—but she loves you; Goodnight, she loves you so much."

"I love you too, Mimi and I miss you so much. Thank you for everything. I forgive you," I whispered to the air around me.

Knowing we didn't have much time, Finn and I drew each other close and kissed—softly at first, then harder. Electric passion flowed between us.

Hot tears slipped from my eyes, and his too, but we didn't pull away, not wanting to let go, not wanting to be saying goodbye.

As much as losing Finn was going to hurt, I'd had something that no one else in the world did—extra time to love and be loved by him. I couldn't complain about losing him now when everyone else already had.

Our kisses became gentle again, measured, and sweet, but salty too. Finn slowly pulled away and wiped my tears away with his thumbs, allowing his own tears to fall freely.

"Why does it feel like we're at the end of a movie about to say our final, cliché lines?" I intended to laugh but choked on a sob instead.

"They may sound cliché, but it doesn't make them any less true. Give me all the cheese you've got, and I'll do the same."

"Now, I don't know what to say," I said.

"I love you, Claire Goodnight," He put his arms around me and held me close. I rested my head against his chest, listening to the fast beat of his heart—attempting to store the sound in my memory forever.

I imagined we were back at the park on our first date, just beginning instead of ending.

I wasn't sure words existed to describe how much I had come to love him. And if they did exist, I had no idea which order to place them in to make them add up to all that he meant to me.

"You are forever etched on my heart," I said.

"As long as you have room to let others in, there's nowhere else I'd rather be," he said.

"If you can look people up when you get wherever you're going…"

"You can bet Mimi will introduce me to your dad and Sophia. I'll send them your love," he said. "And many, many years from now, I plan on seeing you again."

"I'm counting on that," I said.

Behind him, a sliver of moon hung, weightless, like a swing without chains, floating among a sea of white stars, as if waiting.

"What did you wish for that day in the dandelion field, Goodnight?"

"Love," I said.

"Did it come true?"

After Mimi died and before Finn, I'd kept love away, not believing I was worthy of it. The magic of our second chance changed the trajectory of my life, lifting my turtle shell and opening the wings of my heart.

"Yes! Everything is different now—I have more love than I ever imagined I could," I said.

Somewhere between dandelions and birthday cake candles, Mimi had been able to make my wish for Finn come true and had given me more than I knew to ask for. I had Julia and Tyler, as well as, grandparents, an uncle, and cousins to meet. I also had the hope of a mom in Lisa now.

I wouldn't doubt the magic of the universe again.

Finn began to shiver.

Now, the moment I'd been dreading since Finn's ghost had knocked me over with his excitement—just like he had in kindergarten—was here—I had to let him go.

I placed my arms around his neck, lacing my fingers together, aiming to steady him and keep him there a little longer. He wrapped his arms around me and pulled me into him.

We pressed our noses together and simultaneously whispered, "I love you."

Then, as if magnetized, our lips met in a kiss that both held on and let go. He slowly began to disappear from my arms, until he was once again, just a hazy light that I could see through.

His eyes stayed on mine until all that remained were specks of light that began to separate and turn into what looked like dandelion puffs, dancing their way into the endless night sky.

The ache of missing Finn was instant and something I would feel for the rest of my life, but I would be okay.

As I drove home, the last splintered pieces of my heart shifted back together—making space for more love and new beginnings.

Somewhere Between Dandelions Playlist (Spotify)

https://spoti.fi/42fnfLa

1. Last Kiss (Taylor's Version) | Taylor Swift
2. The Hardest Thing | Tyler Ward
3. Middle of the Night Mind | Kate Voegele
4. Stone (feat. Sebastian Kole) | Alessia Cara
5. Only Hope | Switchfoot
6. All I've Ever Needed | AJ Michalka
7. Every Second | Kari Kimmel
8. Meant to Be (Acoustic) | Bebe Rexha
9. Say Love | James TW
10. You & I One Direction
11. Midnight Flight | Canyon City
12. Why Don't You Love Me (feat. Demi Lovato) | Hot Chelie Rae
13. Rescue | Lauren Daigle
14. Control | Zoe Wees
15. Rescue | Tyler James Bellinger
16. Midnight (feat. Liam Payne) | Alesso
17. Love Me Anyway (feat. Chris Stapleton) | Pink
18. Marjorie | Taylor Swift
19. Anyone | Justin Bieber
20. Sorry | Sheppard
21. If You Love Her | Forest Blakk

ACKNOWLEDGMENTS

The first person I need to acknowledge is my mom, Sherry. Mom, you were always open to me following my dreams and never once questioned my choice to major in Creative Writing. You never once told me that writing probably wouldn't pay the bills. You let me find my own path and I'm beyond grateful for that. Your unwavering support of me as your daughter, a person, and a writer has shaped who I am today. Thank you for all you have done for me. You are my mom, friend and soulmate combined into one.

To my sisters, Krista, Brittany, and Brooke, I'm grateful I get to walk through life with you. Thank you for always supporting my heart-finding ways.

To my dad, Jack, thank you for loving me as I am. And to my stepmom, Sandy, thanks for being one of my biggest cheerleaders and for taking care of Dad! I'm happy to have you both in my life.

To my grandfather, Swen Larson, it is my connection to you and our family history that led me to include my maiden name, Larson, on the cover of this book. You loved me unconditionally, and even though you're no longer here, I don't have to wonder if I have made you proud because I know in my heart that I have.

To my children, Zoey and Hunter, you are and always will be my heart walking outside of my body. May you be inspired to follow your dreams as you watch me kick the butt out of mine. I love you both more than you will ever know.

To my many nephews and nieces, Brody, Bailey, Bentley, Brickley, Piper, Kaia, and Caylee—I love watching you grow and change and I'm excited to see all the amazing things you will do.

Joe, thank you for helping me create two of the best humans in the world and for always believing in me as a writer.

I most definitely wouldn't have completed this journey to publication without the help of Kathy Derrick and her Pen to Paper writing program. Working with you gave my novel the reboot and rejuvenation it needed. You noticed my poetic voice and pushed me to dig deeper and it made all the difference.

To Melissa Drake, when you gifted me with a dandelion necklace a couple of years ago, I had no idea that you'd one day help me publish my book! I'm grateful the universe placed you on my path. Thank you for introducing me to Sean Cardinalli, who edited and made excellent points concerning revisions.

An immense thank you goes out to all the friends and family members who have read the many versions of this book over the years. I can't name you all, but you know who you are! I appreciate your enthusiasm and support for me and this story.

Thank you, Thomas, for your best friendship over the years and unintended inspiration for this novel.

None of this would've been possible without my lovely characters, Claire and Finn. You are etched in my heart forever, and I can't wait for the world to meet you.

I've spent hours thinking, dreaming, writing, and editing this book—and it was worth every second. My dream of being a published writer has come true. I have made my past, current, and future selves proud. I'm full of gratitude for this experience and for all the great things to come.

AUTHOR BIO

Trisha Larson Harmon was born and raised in Redlands, California. She has been passionate about writing since a young age. She obtained her BA from UC Riverside and her MFA from CSU Long Beach, both in creative writing. She is also certified as a spiritual life coach. She resides in Los Alamitos, California with her daughter and son. *Somewhere Between Dandelions* is her first novel.

You can connect with Trisha at her website, trishaharmon.com

www.ingramcontent.com/pod-product-compliance
Lightning Source LLC
Chambersburg PA
CBHW061244310726
48971CB00007B/2218